BLAST

A figure poppe[...] those spring-loade[...] out at a child. Lon[...] side of the house where he was standing. A spray of buckshot splintered the dried-out wood, stinging Longarm's wrist but doing no harm. The sonuvabitch was quick. Lordy, he was quick. He had fired and was skeedaddling for cover about as quick as a man could blink. Longarm snapped a shot at him, but couldn't tell if he connected or not . . .

TABOR EVANS

LONGARM

AND THE
LAST MAN

JOVE BOOKS, NEW YORK

LONGARM AND THE LAST MAN

A Jove Book / published by arrangement with
the author

PRINTING HISTORY
Jove edition / April 1994

ISBN: 0-515-11356-5

A JOVE BOOK®
Jove Books are published by The Berkley Publishing Group,
200 Madison Avenue, New York, New York 10016.
JOVE and the "J" design are trademarks
belonging to Jove Publications, Inc.

PRINTED IN THE UNITED STATES OF AMERICA

10 9 8 7 6 5 4 3 2 1

LONGARM

AND THE
LAST MAN

Chapter 1

Longarm crossed his legs, uncrossed them, leaned back in his chair and yawned, and crossed his legs again. He wasn't bored exactly. But he wasn't real far from it either. It didn't help that he was getting hungry now. He'd spent his lunch hour getting a haircut at a new shop over on Sheridan near the State Capitol Building that was the centerpiece of downtown Denver. But that had been a mistake. The barber obviously intended to cater to the desires of rich legislators, not working guys like Longarm. He charged fifty cents for a haircut. And over and above that thoroughly outrageous fee, he chattered incessantly about politics while he snipped. Longarm had no interest whatsoever in politics of any stripe or flavor, but a dandy who was waiting to be chopped on sure did. He and the barber got to talking, and it had taken damn near the entire hour before Longarm could get out of that chair and make his way back here to Billy Vail's office in the Federal Building.

U.S. Marshal Vail had left word that morning that he wanted to see his number-one deputy—well, number-one by Longarm's somewhat prejudiced designation—immediately after lunch. That meant Longarm hadn't been able to sneak in some extra time for a quick sandwich or some eat-and-run pastries on his way back. He'd hurried straight from the barbershop to Billy's office.

And now here he sat with his stomach growling. Billy wasn't back from his own lunch as yet.

Longarm sighed and tried to quell the intestinal revolt with a smoke. He pulled out one of his slim cheroots, an extra-fancy grade with a pale wrapper and excellent-quality filler tobacco, and carefully nipped the twist off the end of it, spitting the bit of surplus tobacco into his palm after he did so. He flicked the twist end in the direction of the cuspidor placed beside Billy's big desk, then dipped two fingers into a vest pocket to extract a sulfur-tipped wooden match. The matches shared that pocket with the tag end of a gold chain that crossed his belly from one pocket to the other. One side of that chain was attached to the expected pocket watch, in this case a railroad-grade Ingersoll. The other end, however, did not hold the usual watch key. Instead that end of the inoffensive-seeming chain was soldered to a small but powerful .44-caliber derringer with a brass frame and a big bite. In Longarm's line of work, which had to do with crooks, crime, and the privilege of continued life and freedom, he'd found use for the hideout gun more than once in days past.

He sat for a few minutes enjoying the flavor of the cheroot. The smoke was indeed helping to hold the hunger pangs at bay.

Not even a good cigar, though, can do much to send impatience packing. There still was no sign of Billy Vail.

Longarm stood and paced about the marshal's office, stopping now and then to tap ashes into a marble ashtray on Billy's desk.

He would have gone through the papers on the desk without qualm . . . except there weren't any. Billy kept his desktop bare and barren, innocent of anything that prying eyes might find. Darn it.

Once Longarm paused to examine himself in the decorative mirror that hung on the wall over the cabinet that Longarm knew, innocent appearances to the contrary, held a small but select stock of beverages.

He examined the results of the talkative barber's efforts, and reluctantly admitted that the so-and-so could cut hair pretty well.

But then, at fifty cents a visit the guy ought to cut hair, sing, and maybe dance a few steps too.

Longarm turned his head this way and that, trying to find something to complain about. He couldn't. At least not anything that the barber was responsible for. As for the rest of it, well, he supposed he had no real kick coming there either.

His hair and eyes were brown, and he had a sweeping, handlebar mustache to match. His face was deeply tanned by wind and weather, and to him seemed on the wrinkled and craggy side, certainly nothing of great interest or importance.

On the other hand, a good many persons of the female persuasion seemed to find his looks fetching enough. That was something he was willing to acknowledge without conceit. And to appreciate whenever the results warranted.

Apart from what he could see in the mirror, Longarm was of better than average height, measuring some inches over six feet in stocking feet. He had a horseman's lean build, with narrow hips and broad shoulders. His hands were powerful, with long fingers that were comfortable when wrapped around the butt of the double-action .44 Colt revolver he carried in a cross-draw holster just to the left of his belt buckle. He wore a tweed coat, calfskin vest, and checked flannel shirt with a string tie loosely knotted at his throat. His trousers were brown corduroy. His gunbelt and stovepipe cavalry boots were black. A snuff-brown Stetson hat with a low, flat crown lay on the floor beside the chair he'd been occupying.

He cleared his throat and leaned close to the mirror. By damn he'd been right. A single, spiky hair had escaped from the seal-sleek flow of mustache and been left to curl back and up toward his nostril. Why, another fraction of an inch or so of growth and that hair would be tickling the bejabbers out of him. That damn barber should have noticed the hair and snipped it. Now Longarm was going to have to yank it out. The offending follicle was sticking upright at a funny angle, and was growing in an awkward spot to begin with, immediately underneath his nose. He'd have to kind of twist and wiggle some to trap the little SOB between his thumbnail and the nail on his middle finger. He figured he was going to have to get a pretty good grip on the thing to pluck it out, and did his best to get a handle on the situation, scowling and twisting his jaw and probing under his nose with one big hand.

Billy Vail chose that moment to walk in from his lunch.

And he wasn't alone.

"Sam, this is, um, the deputy I was telling you about. Deputy Marshal Custis Long, this is Assistant U.S. Attorney Sam Beckwith."

The government lawyer hesitated about half a heartbeat before he nodded and shoved a hand out for a shake.

Shit, Longarm couldn't blame the guy. It sure had to have looked like he was standing there picking his nose—and admiring himself in the damn mirror while he did it—instead of trying to cull an errant mustache hair.

No point in trying to explain, he realized. He wouldn't be believed anyhow and words would just make it worse. So he settled for making this Beckwith fella feel at least a mite better. Longarm hauled a bandanna out of his back pocket and carefully wiped his hands before he accepted the bravely offered shake. "Pleasure to meetcha, Sam."

"Yes, um, likewise I'm sure."

"Sit down, Longarm, Sam," Billy put in. "Let's get down to business, shall we?"

4

Longarm was plenty willing to do that. He dropped the butt end of his cheroot into Billy's cuspidor and sat like a good little fella, determined to be on his best behavior for the rest of the interview, whatever it proved to be about.

Chapter 2

"Tell me, Longarm, do you happen to know what a Last Man Club is?"

Longarm shrugged. "Sure do, Billy. The way I understand it you can use a bottle, like some real fine whiskey, or a sum of money, most anything you like. You get a bunch of fellas together, comrades from an outfit that fought together or whatever, an' they agree to be pals for life. Maybe they get together now an' then or maybe they don't. Point is, they keep this thing, whatever it is, but they don't none of 'em touch it. It's like . . . a symbol or a talisman. It belongs to the bunch of them, an' no single one of 'em can use it until the rest have died off and there's just one of them left. Then he takes the thing, this bottle of whiskey or chunk of money or whatever, and he uses it in remembrance of his comrades that went before him. And that, the way I've heard it, is pretty much what a Last Man Club is about. Am I right, Billy?"

"Right on the money, Longarm," Vail agreed.

"Nothing against the law in a Last Man Club, is there?" Longarm asked.

"Not a thing," Vail said.

"Normally," Sam Beckwith put in.

Longarm lifted an eyebrow and waited for the lawyer to explain.

"We have something of a—how shall I put this?—a situation. It, ahem, involves a Last Man Club. Or at least we believe that it does."

"Yes?"

"The thing is . . ." Beckwith stood and began to pace the room, his nervous energy making Billy Vail's office seem considerably smaller than it really was. "The thing is, Long, there is a Last Man Club of officers, and former officers, of the United States Army. Oh, I am sure there are a great many such groups involving military officers, and perhaps even some among enlisted men as well."

Longarm didn't have any trouble figuring out that Samuel Beckwith must once have been an officer himself. Because why else would he qualify the statement that enlisted men had feelings that would lead them to want to have Last Man Clubs as well? Longarm kept quiet, though, and let the lawyer talk.

"This particular group consists of officers who served together in the forts along the old Bozeman Trail back in the late '60s. Are you familiar with the period in question?"

"Some," Longarm drawled. "That's the bunch that got whipped by Red Cloud an' his Sioux."

Beckwith's face colored, starting out pink and progressing through various shades of salmon, red, ocher, and scarlet until it approached plum purple. Longarm kind of found the transformation interesting.

"By God, sir, you will withdraw that scurrilous remark at once or I shall . . . shall . . . Marshal Vail, please remind your employee to be quiet on subjects he knows nothing about." Without waiting for Billy's response, Beckwith bulled forward. "There was no defeat of those fine young men," he snapped. "Far from it. If they had been allowed to do what they were fully capable of doing . . ."

7

Beckwith paused for a moment and Longarm, in a tone of feigned innocence, observed, "But wasn't that fella—what was his name again? Oh, yeah, Fetterman, that's it. Didn't that Captain Fetterman get exactly the chance he asked for?"

Longarm hoped Sam Beckwith had a safety pop-off valve built into his gizzard, for otherwise he just might puff up past his limits and explode.

"Bill Fetterman was a hero. A hero, I tell you. He died in valor, a martyr to the treachery of the red man."

Longarm gave Billy Vail a sideways glance and decided to let that one go by without comment.

The truth, of course, was that this Captain Fetterman— William, a name which Longarm had forgotten over the years but which Sam Beckwith certainly remembered well enough— had been a blowhard and, at least the way Longarm understood it, something of an asshole. And worse, an unlucky blowhard and asshole.

Fetterman had been serving at one of the Bozeman Trail forts—Fort Phil Kearny, if Longarm remembered correctly— during what was now known as the Red Cloud War. Brash and boastful, Captain Fetterman was fond of claiming that with eighty men he could cut a path clean through the entire Sioux Nation and give those Indians the thrashing they so soundly deserved.

Then sometime in the winter of—Longarm tried to remember—'66? '67? He thought it was somewhere around Christmas-time in one of those years when a wood-cutting detail came under attack by the Sioux. A relief expedition was mounted to chase off the Indians and escort the wood wagons back to the post. Captain Fetterman demanded the right to lead the relief column even though another officer had been initially ordered to command that body. Fetterman's demand was met, and he set out with firm orders that he was to run the Indians off but under no circumstances was he to pursue them, just in case the lightly manned attack on the woodcutters was a ruse.

The relief column started out at once, seventy-eight enlisted men and Captain William Fetterman serving as the officer in command. By a curious quirk of fate two civilians had asked to ride with the column, thus giving Fetterman the exact number, eighty, with which he'd so often sworn he could lick the whole Sioux Nation.

The way Longarm heard it afterward, Fetterman found it easy to run the attacking Sioux off. The Sioux ran, and he gave chase. They ran over a distant ridge, taunting the soldiers and making rude gestures at them.

Fetterman's orders had been clear. Relieve the wood train and return without a running chase. Except that this was the blowhard's opportunity to prove how inferior those ignorant savages were. And, the reverse of that coin, what a dandy officer William Fetterman was.

So ignoring the orders issued by his commanding officer, Fetterman and his eighty men rode over the top of that ridge and out of sight from the fort.

They rode into a beehive conceived and constructed by perhaps the greatest war chief the Sioux Nation ever had, Red Cloud.

Not one of the men was ever seen alive again. Except, that is, by the Sioux who were waiting in ambush beyond—the name of the place was coming back to Longarm now—Lodge Trail Ridge.

Captain Fetterman and his entire command were massacred that day in an event that was, until the debacle at the Little Big Horn some ten years later, the second worst massacre ever experienced by United States military troops.

And personal loyalties aside, Longarm still didn't see how anyone could claim that William Fetterman was anything but a blowhard and an asshole, judging by the performance he'd left written in the pages of his nation's history.

Longarm realized all that, but for Billy Vail's sake managed to hold his tongue. "You were sayin' something about a Last

Man Club, sir?" was all he said aloud.

"Yes, uh, so I was." Beckwith continued to frown, but after a few moments his color returned to normal. "So I was, yes." He paused in his pacing and pointed toward the cabinet where Billy kept a few bottles for the comfort of visitors. Obviously Sam Beckwith was not a stranger to this office.

"Gentlemen," Vail injected, taking the hint. "What will it be? Bourbon for you, Sam? Longarm, why don't you pour for us all, please. You know what I like."

Longarm did as he was told, giving Beckwith a tumbler of bourbon whiskey, pouring a small Madeira for Billy—the boss was trying to cut back—and taking a tot of Billy's first-rate Maryland distilled rye for himself. The air, not just the palate, seemed a little clearer for the break.

Sam Beckwith helped himself to a second bourbon and then resumed his explanation. "To return to the point at hand here," he said, "at about that time, indeed some months before the tragedy involving Bill Fetterman, there was formed a Last Man Club among some of the younger officers assigned duties at the Bozeman Trail forts.

"And before you ask, Long, no, I myself was not a party to this. Although I would have been had things worked out a little differently. You see, we all—those young officers, myself, a few others—had been friends and comrades in arms since before the Southern rebellion. We, most of us, were classmates at the Military Academy at West Point. We served through the conflict and most of us were breveted to rather high rank. Then, of course, after the war the size of the army was reduced. We all reverted to our true rank, mostly that of first lieutenant, a few of us as captains. Most of our particular little group wound up in those Bozeman Trail forts. I myself took a different path. During the war I had had occasion to act as prosecutor, or in several instances jurist, on a number of courts-martial. I discovered an affinity for the law and if I do say so, an aptitude for it. The army granted me an extended leave of absence so I could read law and become qualified to join the Judge Advocate General Corps. Which I subsequently did, and served a number of years in that organization. Later on I resigned my commission to accept a position with the Justice Department, but that is neither here nor there at the moment."

"Right," Longarm prompted. "You were telling me about this Last Man Club your friends put together."

"Exactly." Beckwith tossed off his bourbon and looked around for another. Billy Vail obliged him while Beckwith resumed his story. "Where was I? Oh, yes. As you may appreciate, the group's ranks began to diminish soon after the club was formed. The final member, the last survivor as it were, will be a wealthy man once all is said and done. There were twenty members in the club to begin with, each of them young officers of quality and breeding, and each man contributed one thousand dollars. Cash. The money was placed into a trust account, at a bank owned by one of the young gentlemen's fathers if it matters, and has been drawing interest ever since at the rate of one and seven eighths percent per annum. The principal amount has already become, well, to put it mildly, a sum of considerable substance."

Longarm grunted. That was, like the gent implied, a hell of a bundle, all right. Twenty thousand. Plus whatever the accumulated interest was. And the interest on top of that interest. Anyway, he was sure it all added up to a snootful.

"In any event, the club was formed and the money put on deposit along with a letter of instruction that it be released to the last man living. It was to be this survivor's duty to call together a group of young West Point graduates and tell them the story of these officers who had gone before them. Then all, including the last man, would raise their glasses in honor of the departed. It was intended that part of the money be used to finance that party. The rest, of course . . ." Beckwith shrugged. "I suppose it sounds rather sentimental now, but at

11

the time . . ." Beckwith's voice died away and he turned to cough into his fist.

When he turned back he said, "Bill Fetterman was a member of the club. I believe he was the first of them to die. Two more perished at the Little Big Horn. Another died with Crook on the Rosebud, and Joseph's Nez Percé cut down another young and gallant officer. R.C. Queen succumbed to a fever in the jungles of Panama, and Harold Snow died in a mining accident in the Sierra Nevada. I knew them all. They were my brothers."

Beckwith reached for another bourbon. Longarm shot a questioning glance toward Billy, but Billy pretended not to see it.

"To make a long story short, most survived until quite recently. Then there began a series of murders. It seems . . . oh, God . . . it seems someone is systematically going down the list of names, in the exact order as inscribed on the membership roll, murdering these fine and gallant men."

"And you don't know who is doing it or why?" Longarm asked.

"Oh, but that is part of the tragedy," Sam Beckwith said. "I am sure I do know exactly who is doing this. And why."

Chapter 3

"Tell me, Long, does the name Ellis Reese mean anything to you?" Beckwith asked. "Major Ellis Reese?"

Longarm fingered his chin and gave the name some thought—obviously this wasn't any casual question the government lawyer was asking—but for all his cogitating he nonetheless came up empty. "No, sir, I can't say that I've ever heard of the gentleman."

"You are sure about that, Deputy?"

Longarm commenced to bristle just a mite. "I said so, didn't I?"

Billy Vail gave Beckwith a look of warning and, perhaps pointedly, set his empty wine glass down with a clearly audible thump, as if maybe he was silently suggesting to Beckwith that the lawyer lay off the booze and pay attention to business. At least that was the way Longarm chose to read it. He could've been wrong, he supposed.

"Yes, well, Major Reese was the subject of a scandal some years back. This was a few months before the Rosebud and Little Big Horn battles, back in the late winter of '76. February, if it matters."

"Yes, sir," Longarm said in response to Beckwith's stare.

Apparently some form of response was wanted, although Longarm didn't know what.

"You still don't recall?"

"No, sir." Longarm decided against telling this self-important lawyer that the army and its scandals simply weren't high on his list of things to fret about. Not nowadays, and not back in February of '76 either.

"Yes, well, those who pay attention to events will naturally recall that this Major Reese was the subject of a Congressional investigation and the, um, resulting court-martial. Reese was in charge of the procurement of supplies for Indian reservations within General Terry's command. It was discovered that payment was being made for hay, grains, and certain human consumables that were never delivered to the intended destinations. Invoices were presented and approved and payment was issued, but the supplies were never in fact delivered. Even transportation charges were paid on these nonexistent materials. The amount of loss very likely mounted into the tens of thousands of dollars. For the purposes of prosecution, however, specific accounts totaling slightly over seven hundred dollars were detailed and formal charges were filed against Major Reese."

"You were a part of the prosecution?" Longarm guessed.

"I was not, sir. Now may I finish relating this, or would you care to turn it into a cross-examination?"

"Sorry," Longarm said, not particularly meaning it.

"I see I am boring you, Deputy, so I'll make this short. Major Reese was convicted of misappropriation of government funds, was stripped of rank and privilege, and was sentenced to a fifteen-year term of incarceration in the federal penitentiary at Fort Leavenworth, Kansas."

That sure sounded like the end of the yarn to Longarm. And a mighty uninteresting one at that. But he knew better than to say so out loud. Not that he gave a damn about making Lawyer Beckwith mad, but it wouldn't reflect well on Billy. And

Longarm would go a long way to keep from doing anything that would be disrespectful of Billy Vail.

"Between time off for good behavior and in view of certain, um, considerations of health, I am given to understand that Ellis Reese will be released from prison sometime within the next six months—that is to say, shortly after the next sitting of the Board of Pardons."

"And that has somethin' to do with the Last Man Club?" Longarm suggested.

"Of course it does, man. What the hell d'you think I've been getting at here?"

Longarm looked briefly at Billy and kept his mouth shut. Damn, but he did feel noble about that.

"Ellis Reese is going to be released from prison sometime later this year. And if things keep on going the way they have been, he will walk out of the cell a rich man, thanks to the contributions made by his betters."

Longarm did go so far as to lift an eyebrow.

"Reese was one of the original members of the club, of course. And unfortunately, there is nothing in the letter of instruction that disqualifies him from receiving the money if he should be the last living member of the group. Not that the gentlemen didn't try to have him removed from the list at the time, of course. After all, he'd proven himself completely unworthy. He was a disgrace to the uniform and to his fellows, and everyone involved wanted him out. There was considerable effort invested toward that end, but the hidebound old fart in charge of the trust refused to listen to reason. And naturally, Reese himself was not gentleman enough to voluntarily withdraw himself. He became quite abusive, in fact. Kept claiming innocence—they all do, don't they?—and muttering darkly about supposed deceptions by his brother officers. Harrumph! Have you ever heard of such nerve, I ask you. Of course the prosecution had him dead to rights. I reviewed the case myself, just to make sure. The testimony left no room for doubt. None whatsoever. Ellis Reese violated the trust placed in him by his nation. Worse, he violated the trust and the respect of his brother officers. And now . . . now this damned Reese stands to walk away free and wealthy."

"I don't think I understand quite all of the problem here," Longarm injected.

"No?" Beckwith blinked rapidly and, his mouth hanging slightly open, swayed back and forth just a wee bit. "What is it that you don't understand, dammit?"

Billy stood and came around his desk to touch Beckwith's elbow and gently point the man back to his chair. Then Longarm's boss continued the explanation.

"There have been a series of murders, Longarm."

"Yeah, I think I remember somebody sayin' something about that. But it's been kinda a long while back. Some time since then we've taken some forks in the path. You know?"

"Back to the point then, eh?" Billy said agreeably. "The fact of the matter is that these officers and former officers have been dying. Been killed, actually. It was some time before anyone made the connection between these murders and the list of Last Man Club members. Unfortunately. We might have been able to warn some of the gentlemen in time to avert tragedy had anyone realized. As it is . . ." Billy spread his hands and frowned.

"Boss, surely now you ain't gonna tell me that this Reese fella is involved in the murders. Not an' him in Leavenworth all this time."

"No, of course I'll suggest no such thing, Longarm. But there is reason to believe that Ellis Reese's son Steven is very much involved."

"Oh?"

"Steven was in his early teens when his father was convicted and sent to prison. The boy has grown up since then. Hired out to a Texas trail crew and learned how to take care of himself. By all accounts, he has become a hard and competent man.

16

Yet he remains a devoted son. Twice a year, more often if he can manage it, he visits his father in prison. He is said to be a *very* devoted and dutiful son."

"Dammit, Billy, I don't care if this guy runs a home for unwed mothers an' qualifies for sainthood. Just what does all this shit have to do with a bunch of army officers gettin' themselves killed?"

"Ellis Reese is dying, Longarm. He contracted consumption sometime ago, and the latest report is that now he has a cancerous growth in the bowel as well. The army doctors at Leavenworth say he will barely live long enough to see freedom."

"And?"

"And his son Steven apparently believes that if there is money enough to pay for the treatment, Ellis Reese can be operated on in an attempt to excise the tumor. There is a doctor in Scotland who claims—"

"A quack," Beckwith put in. "A charlatan."

Longarm gave the lawyer a hooded look. As far as he could tell to this point, if all Ellis Reese needed to fully recover was a sugar tit, Samuel Beckwith would do his damnedest to see that the disgraced West Pointer never got it.

"As I was saying," Billy continued, "there is a doctor who claims he can help. Regardless of whether he can produce a miracle or not, Steven Reese believes that he can. Or at least that he might. But the costs of the trip and the surgery would be prohibitive."

"Unless his daddy was to come into twenty-odd thousand dollars about the time he was gettin' outa prison?" Longarm put in.

"In a word . . . yes," Billy Vail said.

"So you reckon this Steven Reese is goin' around popping his daddy's old comrades between the horns an' making sure that Papa is the Last Man?"

"Yes, exactly."

"Do we have proof?"

"Not actually. Not enough to arrest the young man on."

"Yet," Beckwith said. "Yet." He'd refilled his glass and was sucking the contents down.

"Let's say for the sake of argument that you're right as rain here an' young Steve Reese has become a systematic murderer for the sake of his dear papa," Longarm said. "It looks to me like what we have is plain murder an' therefore a state crime. Or crimes. Whatever."

Because the truth was that murder was not against federal law. And in the absence of a specific request for assistance from some local government or law enforcement agency, United States marshals and their deputies were not supposed to concern themselves with murder and other crimes that fell outside the scope of their jurisdiction.

"Assault on a federal peace officer is ours," Billy said.

"Yeah? So?"

"So the man who should be next on the list is a former army officer who after he resigned his commission worked briefly as a federal deputy in Cincinnati."

"Cincinnati?"

"Um, yes."

"What the hell does that have to do with—"

"As far as we can determine, Longarm, his commission was never revoked by Marshal Hetherington."

"An' that means—"

"That means that, technically speaking, he is still a federal employee, albeit one who hasn't drawn actual pay in, um, some years."

"Hell, none of the rest of us does neither," Longarm mumbled. "Not enough to matter, anyhow."

"Longarm!" Billy admonished.

"Yes, sir. Sorry."

"The thing is, Longarm, we . . . I . . . want you to find this Last Man Club member and, well, warn him. Protect him too if need be."

"You want Steve Reese brought in?"

"If there is cause to arrest him, of course we would expect an arrest to be made."

"But there ain't no warrant outstanding," Longarm said.

"I'm working on it," Beckwith said, his voice husky with liquor.

"Yeah, I'm sure you are at that," Longarm said, his expression bland, never mind his thoughts. Those were private, and he figured he was entitled to them.

"This last fella, you wanta tell me about him, Billy?"

"His name is Harry Bolt."

Longarm grunted. Ellis Reese he'd never heard of. Harry Bolt on the other hand . . .

"The last I heard he was down around Trinidad," Billy said. "Do you know anything more recent than that?"

"Trinidad, Aguilar, somewhere down around there. That's the last I heard too."

"Find him, Longarm. Deliver the warning and . . . do what you can about this Reese thing, will you? There are only a few more men left on the list. It would be a shame for them to die if there is anything we can do to prevent those murders. Right?"

Longarm glanced at Sam Beckwith. He didn't much care for the lawyer. But that sure as hell didn't make it right that more innocent men should die.

"I'll do whatever I can to stop this thing, Billy."

"Good, Longarm. Thank you."

Longarm retrieved his hat from the floor beside his chair and excused himself. He needed to see Billy's clerk Henry about travel vouchers and maybe an advance against expenses. And there wasn't any reason he'd want to stay and chat with Sam Beckwith, that was for sure.

"G'day, gentlemen," Longarm said as he legged it out the door.

Chapter 4

The town was called Picketwire, named in a roundabout fashion for the river that was often miscalled the same. The river's real name had started out in Spanish as River of Lost Souls. That later on became the French word for purgatory, *purgatoire,* and that, corrupted into saddlebag English, became picketwire. Hence the town of Picketwire.

Longarm had reached it by way of a Denver and Rio Grande passenger coach south to Trinidad and a stagecoach east to Picketwire. As an officer of the United States government, his badge had let him travel free on the stagecoach since the express company had a government contract to carry official mail. The trip east from Trinidad had been free of charge but not free from complaint. The way the coach driver had carried on about the loss of a three-dollar fee, a body would've thought the price of the ticket was coming out of the driver's own pocket instead of that of the Watson Express line.

"Here," the driver now snapped curtly, an instant before he launched Longarm's carpetbag into the air.

Longarm managed to snag his bag before it hit, but he wasn't quick enough to also grab the saddle that followed. His McClellan, complete with scabbarded Winchester, hit the ground with a resounding thump heavy enough to raise a cloud of dark red dust.

"If you've gone an' busted anything o' mine . . ." Longarm started out. But the coach driver wasn't paying him any mind. By then the sour-tempered son of a bitch was carefully, oh-so-carefully, handing a wooden crate down to a drummer who'd also been on the run out from Trinidad. Longarm knew, because the man had mentioned it often enough, that the drummer dealt in ready-made ironwork, things like cabinet hinges and mortise locks and other unbreakable shit of that nature. Yet the damned coachman handled the crate of iron bits like they were fine china, and threw Longarm's valuables around like he hoped they would bust.

Longarm scowled at the man, but decided against trying to teach the jackass any manners. After all, he was supposed to stop problems, not make new ones.

He shouldered his saddle, picked up his bag, and gave some thought to what he should do next. It was late afternoon and there would be time enough later to find a room if it turned out he would be needing one in Picketwire, he decided. Whether he did or not would pretty much depend on what he learned about Harry Bolt and where he was working lately.

Learning that was what Longarm had come to Picketwire to discover.

He carried his things inside the Watson Express Company office, and secured a promise from the clerk there that his gear would be safe behind the counter.

"I'll see to it personally," the young man in sleeve garters and a green celluloid eyeshade assured him.

"I'm obliged," Longarm said. He grinned and added, "Just make sure your jehu don't get another crack at my stuff. He did his darndest to mash everything once, but that was when he had a moving target so the carpetbag had a sportin' chance. I'd hate to see him get lucky the second time."

The clerk laughed. "I'll tell Tom to please keep his distance."

"Like I said, neighbor, I'm obliged."

"Anything for a customer, mister."

Longarm concluded it might be wise to let that one go without clarifying the point. He wasn't a customer exactly. Not a paying one anyhow. He settled for touching the brim of his Stetson in a silent salute and getting out of the stagecoach office before the driver, Tom, came inside.

Longarm stopped on the porch outside to light a cheroot and get his bearings—after all, it had been quite a while since he'd been down this way—then strode off toward the west end of the town, down along the sluggish and at times nearly nonexistent river that gave Picketwire its name.

When he reached his destination he grunted softly under his breath. The place hadn't changed much since the last time he'd been there. The peeled log walls had maybe weathered a little more, and the chinks between the logs had sprung maybe a bit wider. The gaps were too big to ignore, and someone was going to have to do some serious mud-daubing before winter or there wouldn't be a stove made that'd be capable of keeping the place heated.

Still, it didn't look all that bad. The building rambled this way and that, taking off from a central core little bigger than a homesteader's cabin, and showing the numerous additions that'd been added on since that first structure was thrown together.

There was a lean-to on the right end that he didn't think had been there before, and now there was a stout corral where before there'd only been hitching posts and a flimsy hayrick. Apart from those things, though, it still looked pretty much the way he last remembered it.

Longarm stood in the shelter of a cottonwood tree for a few moments while he finished his cheroot. Then he ground the stub of the cigar under the heel of his boot and, taking a deep breath, ambled inside the saloon, general store, and whatever else it might be.

"You again," the barman said with an undertone of annoyance, sounding the way he might have if an unwelcome regular was stopping in for the third time on the same afternoon. It had been, Longarm remembered, something over two years since he'd last been underneath this roof.

"Nice to see you too, Gregory."

"There's a new saloon in town," Gregory suggested. "Nice place. I think you'd like it. It's up on Main Street. The Bob Dwyer, run by a guy named Bob though his last name ain't Dwyer. Cute, huh? I'm sure you'll like the place."

"Thanks, Gregory, but I expect I'll stay here for the time bein'."

"Rye whiskey then?"

"That'd be fine."

Gregory produced a dust-covered jug and pulled the cork. He tipped a generous slug of the aged whiskey into a glass and pushed it across the bar.

"I'm impressed," Longarm said, lifting the glass and judiciously smelling the aroma before taking a small taste and allowing the liquor to lie warm on his tongue for a moment before he swallowed. "This is your good stuff."

"I want you satisfied and quick as possible out of here," Gregory said with a level gaze.

Longarm fished a handful of change out of his pocket and laid it onto the counter. Gregory ignored the money. "How much?" Longarm insisted.

"On the house," the barman said. "Just drink up and leave." He hesitated. "Please."

Longarm sighed. He opened his mouth to say something, thought better of the impulse, and closed it. A moment later he said, "I won't be long. This is business, Gregory. Official. I have to ask a couple questions. Then I'll go."

"Anything I can answer?"

"I'm willing to give you the chance," Longarm said. "It's about Harry Bolt, Gregory. I need to find him."

The barman frowned. "You come in on the stage just now?"

"That's right."

"Then you just come down from where I thought Harry was still working. Last thing I heard he was night marshal at Trinidad."

"I talked to the mayor there first thing when I hit town," Longarm said. "He told me Bolt quit the night marshal job there about four, five months back. He said I should ask—"

"Dammit," Gregory hissed. "If it ain't one of you bastards it's the other. I don't know what she sees in you gun-crazy sons of bitches."

Longarm gave the bartender a tight smile. "That's the difference between Harry and me, Gregory. You can say something like that to my face an' know I won't blow a hole through your breastbone for it. You say the same thing to Harry Bolt an' you're a dead man. An' anyway, you know good an' well what she sees in us. It's the smell of gunsmoke an' the excitement of bein' close to the Grim Reaper, Gregory. Not that I agree with any of that, mind. But it's what she thinks she sees, which is enough to make it so."

"Damn you to hell, Custis Long."

Longarm sighed again and finished his rye—it really was prime stuff—and said, "I may well be headed in that direction, Gregory. But lucky for me, that ain't for you to say." He shook his head no when Gregory offered to pour another. "Thanks, but one is enough for right now. Just tell me where I can find her." He looked suggestively toward the wall behind the bar where a doorway had been cut through.

Gregory frowned, but after a moment nodded. "She's there, Long. She's most always there lately."

Longarm raised an eyebrow.

"She hasn't been feeling good, Long. She's been real sick."

"Sick, Gregory? Or . . . ?"

24

"What do you want me to say, Long? She's been sick. Never mind that the sickness comes in a little brown bottle."

"Damn," Longarm said.

"Seeing you will make it worse again, Long."

"I won't say anything that—"

"You won't have to. Don't you understand that? It isn't anything you might say. Hell, I know better than to think you'd hurt her. Not that you'd ever mean to. I give you more credit than that, Long. It's just . . . she sees you and she thinks about . . . you know. She'll think about you and she'll think about Harry Bolt and tomorrow she'll drink two, three bottles of that tincture of opium shit, and for the next week or more she'll be floating on some Chink cloud. You know? She'll be fuzzy as a peach in August and constipated as a turkey buzzard. It'll be another month before she'll be worth a damn again, and even then she'll bust out in tears every so often for just no reason at all. And if you're wondering why I hate to see your ass in here, Long, well, screw you and the horse you rode in on. I reckon now you know."

"I'm sorry, Gregory."

"The worst thing about you, you son of a bitch, is that I know you mean that."

Longarm didn't say anything.

"Go on inside, damn you," Gregory said. "I won't do anything to stop you."

Longarm started toward the end of the bar, then stopped again. "You love her, don't you, Gregory?"

"Get the hell away from me, Long."

Longarm went behind the bar and made his way through the doorway that led to the private living quarters in one of the many ramshackle add-on room sections.

It had been a long time, but he remembered the way very, very well.

Chapter 5

Jesus God! Longarm thought, barely able to stop himself from blurting it aloud.

Emmaline Constance Bertolucci looked . . . awful. Simply awful.

Her flesh was bloated and puffy, and her complexion—oh, that complexion that had been as clear and perfect as the finest porcelain—her complexion was blotchy red and orange and yellow.

She looked fat, except she wasn't fat. It was more like a thin person had been inflated or maybe pumped full of water so that she bulged and protruded in unlikely places.

Her hair—which had been her crowning glory and a source of considerable vanity—was lank and greasy and looked like she'd neither washed nor combed it for weeks or months on end.

Instead of a subtly artful application of fine cosmetics, she had caked her face and neck with layer upon layer of powders, and as they dried the layers had cracked and flaked away, or in some places allowed grime and sweat to accumulate in the crevasses.

Even her eyes, those china blue orbs, were ruined by being surrounded with heavy daubs of black goo that might have been makeup or might have been nothing more exotic than axle grease. Putting crap like that around eyes like Emmaline's was like setting a fine diamond in a bed of drying cat shit.

Longarm felt sickened just from looking at her. At this woman who once—and not so terribly long ago as all that, really—had meant so very much to him.

He tried his best to keep his feelings from being reflected on his face, forcing a smile and a cheery voice. "Hello, Emmy. How've you been?"

"Custis!" she shrieked. "You've come back, Custis!"

"I . . . I've come to visit, Emmy. That's all. Just a visit."

"Oho, Custis dear." She giggled. "Whatever you say, hee-hee." She grinned and simpered and twisted about on the chaise where she was reclining. She batted her eyelashes quite furiously and flopped her hands about. It took him a moment for Longarm to realize that this . . . this creature who had once been his beloved Emmaline was being girlishly coquettish with him.

She leered and giggled and in her contortions managed to make her gown spread apart to display the heavy, blue-veined dugs that Longarm had long ago suckled and teased. And beneath a roll of fat as white as a fish's belly there was a hint of the copper coils of pubic hair that he remembered tickling his nose and the point of his freshly shaved chin. Emmaline then had been as fresh and fragrant as a blossom in springtime. Now he could smell the sour stink of her from across the room.

"It's nice to see you, Emmy."

"I knew you'd come back to me, Custis."

"We don't want to go through all that again, Emmy. We all made our choices a long while back. They seemed the right choices at the time, and it's too late now for regrets or recriminations."

"But not too late to change our minds, is it, Custis?" she said with another flutter of her eyelashes. Longarm felt vaguely ill.

"I didn't . . . I didn't come to talk about that, Emmy."

"No? What did you come to see me about then, Custis?"

It was true that he'd had, buried somewhere in the dark recesses of his mind, some thought that since Harry was no longer in the way . . . but shit, he didn't want to remember those half-formed suppositions. Not now. Not seeing her like this, he didn't.

"I came on business, Emmy."

"Business, Custis? That's all?"

"Yes. Really." It wasn't much of a lie. "You are the only person I can turn to, Emmy. I came to see you because we are old and dear friends and because I knew I could count on you."

"It's Harry then, isn't it, Custis?"

"Yes, but . . ."

"You know I won't do anything to hurt Harry, Custis. Not even after what he did to me."

"Did to you, Emmy? What did Harry do to you?"

The horrid creature who once had been so beautiful drew herself rigid, summoning the remnants of a faded dignity, and said, "We'll not discuss that, if you please."

"No, Emmy. Whatever you say."

"Exactly, Custis. And what I say is that I shall not be untrue. I will tell you nothing that would bring harm to my Harry."

"Nor would I ever ask you to, Emmy. I came here so you could help me keep Harry safe. There is a man who wants to kill him. I have to find Harry so I can warn him."

"Are you being honest with me, Custis?"

"I'm hurt that you would even ask me that, Emmy. You know I've never been anything but honest with you."

"That's true, old dear." She looked a little weepy now. She produced a handkerchief from inside the sleeve of her gown, and used it to mop at her eyes, smearing the cloth with black ooze from her eye makeup and with pink rice powder from her cheeks. She didn't seem to notice, and fortunately could

28

not see the effect the mopping had on her makeup. "Tell me about this threat to my Harry, Custis."

So he told her, briefly sketching the mission Billy Vail had given him.

"And you say Harry is the next target of this young person?"

"That's what the man from the Justice Department believes."

"Harry used to be an officer, you know. An officer and a gentleman."

"Yes, Emmy, I know."

"He had a ring, you know. West Point. And he was a federal deputy too, you know. Before he became the marshal here."

"Yes, I know that, Emmy."

"You were never an officer, Custis. Though you were a gent, hee-hee. Just not by an act of Congress like Harry was."

"That's right, Emmy." It was so silly for her to go on now about inconsequential things like that. Yet the fact of Harry Bolt's having been an officer and a gentleman by act of Congress apparently meant much to Emmaline Bertolucci. Lord, but she was shallow. So much more so than he'd ever realized in the past.

"And you aren't just trying to trick me, are you, Custis? You don't have a warrant for Harry, do you?"

"No, Emmy, I swear to you, it's just the way I said. I need to find him so I can help him, not so I can take him in."

"All right then, Custis. Let me think about this. Maybe I will tell you." She drew back and cackled. "And maybe I won't."

Longarm felt an urge to slap Emmaline across the face, to bring her back to the here and now.

Except, in a manner of speaking, he doubted that she even had been here and now with him. Emmaline seemed to live in her own blurry sphere, and that was a place Longarm did not want to share with her.

"You can call on me again later, Custis." She batted her eyes at him. "We'll talk then. And maybe I'll tell you, maybe

I won't." Her laughter was as loud as a crow's cawing. And held just about the same amount of human warmth or caring.

Longarm shuddered.

But this was Emmaline's mad game. It would be played out by her rules or not at all.

"I'll call on you again later, Emmy. We'll talk again then, yes?"

"Yes, my dear. We'll talk later." Emmaline made cow's eyes at him and twisted about on her chaise so that her pendulous, sweat-shiny breasts were put on display, presumably to arouse his passions.

Longarm felt a great welling of pity for this woman. And a great distaste for her company as well.

He managed a smile, however, bowed low as if paying her court, and backed out of the darkly curtained room.

Jesus, he thought. Jesus, Mary, and Joseph.

Chapter 6

"I hope you'll be leaving now, Long," the bartender said when Longarm came back out into the public room.

"For a bit, Gregory, but I gotta come back again later," Longarm said, explaining as briefly as possible.

The barman grimaced and stood there for a moment staring bleakly off into space. Finally he said, "She wants time to get herself prettied up."

Poor Emmaline was far past the point where any amount of repair would do much good, Longarm thought. But he wasn't cruel enough to say so to this long-suffering sonuvabitch who still loved her.

"Come back in, let's say three hours, maybe four. I'll . . . go help her. Make sure she's feeling at her best. You know." Gregory wasn't looking at Longarm while he spoke. He held himself stiff, as if he were as fragile as a cold cigar ash and might crumple clean away if he was to make a sudden move. "Have yourself some supper . . . whatever . . . an' come back later tonight, why don't you?"

"That'll be fine, Gregory." He paused for a moment. But hell, there really wasn't anything more to say. Sadly he made his way back outside, into the waning afternoon.

31

His hope of making this stop in Picketwire a quick one was shot to hell and gone by now, so he walked back to the stage station.

The pleasant clerk he'd spoken with earlier was nowhere in sight. But the cantankerous coach driver was.

"Excuse me," Longarm said. There was no immediate response so he tried again a little louder. After all, the fellow might be going deaf or some such. Longarm figured that even could explain the sourness of his disposition. "Excuse me?"

The jehu looked up and scowled. "What'd you do, pass wind or somethin'?"

There was something Longarm would like to pass. His fist clean through the cartilage in this idjit's nose, for instance. But he put on a smile anyway and said, "I'm just wanting to pick up my gear."

"Gear? What gear?"

"My saddle and bag. You remember. You took them down off the stage your own self a little while ago."

"Mister, I handle two dozen pieces o' luggage every day. I sure can't call one from another. An' don't tell me what I should oughta remember. All right?"

"Fine. I apologize. Now if you'd just give me my gear . . ."

"You got a claim ticket?"

"Pardon me?"

"A claim ticket. Every passenger gets a claim ticket for his things. Where's yours?"

"I don't have a claim ticket."

"If you rode my coach you did. It's part of your passage ticket. Right there at the bottom."

"But I wasn't issued a regular ticket. As you know perfectly good and well. I traveled on a government pass."

"Mister, if you ain't got a claim ticket then you don't get no baggage. That's the rules."

Longarm's patience was just *real* close to being used up. He could feel the heat in his cheeks and the tightness across his shoulders and down the back of his neck, all the signs that warned him to keep a tight rein on or else he was going to end up hurting this miserable excuse for a . . .

"Tom!" The voice was sharp. And feminine.

Longarm's attention was drawn to the doorway leading into another room. A woman stood there. A young woman. And a damned pretty one. Longarm snatched his hat off, the frustrations of trying to speak with old Tom put completely aside already.

"Why ever are you acting so snippish with the gentleman, Tom?"

The jehu growled and glowered. "The son of a . . . I mean t' say, Miss Lucy, the gentleman here beat you outa the fare down from Trinidad. Flashed some cheap tin instead. It strikes me wrong when somebody thinks he's got the right t' take something for nothing. That's all."

"But he hasn't taken something for nothing, Tom. The government pays us quite well for our express service. If we didn't want the job, and at that price, we didn't have to bid on it. And we all—you included, Tom—knew to begin with that the mail contract includes passenger privileges for anyone traveling on official business." She smiled. "Tell me, Tom. This gentleman would be—what?—the fourth passenger we've had to carry without charge since we won that contract?"

"Um, somethin' like that. Too many, anyhow."

"Get the gentleman's luggage, please, Tom."

"But Miss Lucy, without a claim tick—"

"Tom!" Her voice was no louder this time than it had been before, but now there was an edge in it sharp enough to slice post oak.

"Yes, ma'am."

The jehu gave in and went grumbling out of sight while the young woman came the rest of the way into the station lobby. "I'm sorry, Mister . . . ?"

Longarm remembered his manners and quickly gave her a little bow. "Long, miss. Deputy U.S. Marshal Custis Long."

"A marshal. Really. That's very exciting. I believe we've had a surveyor before and two postal inspectors, but never a marshal before now."

"Only a deputy, miss. A marshal is somebody way up the ladder. Me, I'm just a hired hand trying to do a job."

She smiled again. Longarm wasn't sure, but he kinda thought the room got brighter when she smiled like that.

"What was it you said your name was, miss?"

"I don't believe I did say," she responded with a twinkle in her eyes—and damn pretty eyes they were, Longarm noted, big and bright and gold with green highlights in them—pretending that was all she intended to divulge. After a moment's teasing she added, "If you must know, for your official reports of course, I'm Lucy Watson. I own the Watson Express Company."

"You an' who else, Miss Lucy?" the driver named Tom prompted from the far side of the room where he had reemerged carrying Longarm's saddle and carpetbag.

"Myself and my brother Luke own the line jointly if you want all the details," she amended, casting a steely glance in Tom's direction.

The driver-turned-freight-handler dropped Longarm's gear onto the floor—Longarm wasn't in any position to catch the bag before it hit this time—and with a clearly audible grunt of disapproval disappeared into the back of the building again.

"Something's sure chewing on that man's . . ." Longarm had been about to say backside, but he thought better of it and lamely went on. "On that, uh, man there."

Miss Lucy Watson smiled—Lordy, but she was awful pretty when she did that—and said, "Tom has been with our family quite literally as long as I can remember, Marshal. He worked for our daddy in the store back in Kansas, and in an oil-drilling venture up in Florence when we first came to Colorado. And

34

in all the things Daddy got into afterward."

"Your papa likes to try his hand at different things, does he?" Longarm said with a smile.

"Not so much because he liked it as because he had little choice in the matter. Daddy wasn't a very good businessman. I loved him to pieces, but the truth is that he was a perfectly awful businessman. And a perfectly wonderful daddy. He died just as he was starting this business. The Watson Express Company is all the estate Luke and I had to fall back on." She smiled again. "And really, Luke is no better at business than Daddy was. So it's up to me to make a go of it, which I certainly shall." The smile became a gentle laugh. "With Tom's help, whether I want it or not."

Longarm smiled too. And took a moment to enjoy the sight of this girl. Woman, he supposed she would prefer to be called. He guessed she would be twenty or a bit over that. Well past the first blush of marrying age anyway, but still short of whispered warnings about becoming a spinster.

Lucy Watson was right at five feet tall. She had honey-colored hair that was mostly hidden under a mob cap and a heart-shaped face. She had round apple cheeks and a perky, pointy nose with the tip turned slightly up. Her neck was unusually long and thin. He couldn't tell much about her figure thanks to a duster that she wore over the top of her dress, but her hands were very nicely made, the fingers long and slender and her nails well kept and burnished.

And she had a smile that could outshine any lantern and most chandeliers. That much Longarm was sure of.

"I'm sorry to hear about your papa dying," Longarm said.

"Thank you."

"And if the lack of my passage is threatenin' the future of this coach line . . ."

Lucy Watson threw her head back and laughed.

"Well, I reckon we settled that much," Longarm said.

"Do you accept my apologies then?"

"For your driver an' my luggage, you mean?"

"Yes."

Longarm pursed his lips and thought for a moment, then shook his head. "No, miss, I don't reckon I do."

The laughter died out of the girl's eyes, and she looked worried. "But . . ."

"What I was thinkin'," Longarm said quickly, "was that you could make amends."

"Yes?"

"I only expected to be in town a few hours, but now I find I gotta stay a spell. Till after supper anyhow. An' that means eatin' alone. I'm a man as craves company, miss. Why, it bothers me something terrible to be alone at mealtime. So what I was thinkin' is that . . ."

The girl began to laugh. "Are you asking me to dine with you tonight, Marshal?"

"I am for a fact," he admitted.

"You are very forward on such short acquaintance."

"Yes'm. But like I said, I don't expect to be in town all that long. Reckon I'd best speak up while I still can."

"You are direct. I like that." She dropped her chin a mite so that she was looking up at him past her eyelashes. And he knew right then what her answer was going to be. "There is a cafe two blocks down. The sign out front says Tyrone's Fine Eats. Ask for the mayor's room. I'm sure Elmer and his cronies won't be using it at this hour; it's where the councilmen and their pals have their coffee and crullers every morning and conduct all the town's important business. But like I said, they won't be using it now. There are a few things I need to do first. I'll meet you there in twenty minutes. Fair enough?"

"Fair enough," he agreed. He glanced down at his bag and saddle.

Lucy grinned. "Put them behind the counter. No one will bother them there."

"And the claim ticket?"

Her laughter was bright as a brass bell's note.

She started toward the back of the station, then paused and turned to look at him. "Marshal?"

"Yes?"

"What was it you said your name was again?"

He told her.

That marvelous smile flashed once more. "I won't forget again."

Longarm felt pretty good as he ambled down the street in search of Tyrone's Fine Eats.

Chapter 7

Longarm dropped his napkin onto his plate and, with a belch that was only half hidden behind his palm, pushed his chair back from the table.

"Go ahead and smoke," Lucy offered without waiting to be asked. "I won't mind."

The lady had a hearty appetite, but was not one to be rushed through her meal. She continued to eat while Longarm crossed his legs and brought out a cheroot.

It wouldn't have been polite to stare—although this girl was certainly worth staring at—so Longarm contented himself with looking around the small room where much of the town's civic planning took place.

There wasn't really all that much to see. The place obviously was valued for its function, not its ambiance. The room was small, just large enough to hold a table with six chairs plus a small sideboard where a coffeepot, creamer, and sugar bowl sat on a pewter tray. Ashtrays dotted the table surface, and spittoons were placed strategically along the perimeter of the floor. There was only one door, through which the waiter silently came and went. Apart from that door the walls were plain, unbroken expanses. No windows, grills, or ornaments intruded on the flat planes of pale green paint. All the light in the room came from a hanging doodad—it wasn't fancy enough to be called a chandelier so Longarm didn't know what the right name for it ought to be—of coal oil lamps suspended from the ceiling.

With no windows, not even a transom over the door to open, Longarm suspected the place could get smoky enough to choke a trout when all the city fathers fired up their cigars.

On the other hand, he had to admire their thinking on the subject. Because while it might get thick inside, there wasn't any way anybody outside the room could be listening in on what was going on once that one-and-only door was closed. The walls and the door alike were stout and as good as soundproof, he'd noticed.

About the time Lucy Watson was finishing her meal—a pot roast so tender it almost fell apart from a sharp glance, accompanied by spuds and gravy and plenty of soft, yeasty rolls to mop up the excess gravy—the waiter came in again. "What will you folks have for dessert?" he asked.

"Nothin' for me, thanks. I'm full to the top," Longarm answered.

"Miss Lucy?"

"Not for me either, Ben. But perhaps the gentleman would like a brandy now?" She inclined her head in Longarm's direction.

"No brandy, but a touch o' rye might be nice," Longarm conceded.

"Rye, Ben, and bring the brandy anyway in case the marshal changes his mind. Oh, and is the coffee hot?"

"I'll fetch a fresh pot just in case," the waiter offered.

"Thank you. And Ben. Please make sure no one disturbs us. The marshal and I have to talk about business. Never mind what it is he has to ask me in here. This is all supposed to be entirely secret."

"You can count on me, Miss Lucy. You know I won't say anything to anybody."

"I know that, Ben. Thank you."

There was a distinct sparkle in the pretty lady's eyes after the waiter left. Longarm looked at her and lifted an eyebrow.

Lucy looked back at him. And burst into laughter. "Ben is a dear. He's also a gossip. If I hadn't given him something to tattle on he would have invented something worse. So now he can make up a dandy yarn indeed. Before midnight tonight half the citizens of Picketwire will know that there is a U.S. marshal in town and that he's asking questions that probably have to do with the United States mail. By morning they probably will have worked out if it's mail theft you are investigating or mail fraud."

"We take on theft from the mails, but the Post Office has its own crowd to look into mail fraud."

Lucy smiled. "Do the good people of Picketwire know that?"

"I see what you mean. I—" He was interrupted by Ben's return. The waiter placed a heavy tray on the sideboard, quickly piled the soiled dishes onto the old coffee tray, and then silently disappeared taking the old tray with him.

Lucy winked at Longarm.

And got up to cross the room—it required only a few strides—to draw a stout bolt shut. No one could enter the private room now unless she or Longarm first chose to unbolt the door.

"Mind if I ask what it is we're doin' here? Assuming, that is, that it ain't mail thievery you got in mind."

Lucy's smile was enigmatic. She came around the table to stand beside him, plucked the stub of his cheroot from his fingers, and tossed it into a nearby cuspidor.

She took the hand that had held the cigar and placed it onto one warm, soft breast.

"Dessert," she told him softly.

Longarm decided he might be able to handle dessert this evening after all.

Chapter 8

Lucy Watson turned out to be one of those women who look better naked than clothed, a trait that is far from being universal.

Her flesh was a pale, velvet texture, very white and very soft.

Her breasts were plump and fluid to the touch, shifting without substance when he squeezed them. By the time Lucy was thirty they would sag, and when she was forty they would hang to her waist. But right now they were fine, the skin containing them so tender it was near transparent. Blue veins showed through like so much subsurface lace, and her nipples were sharp-tipped and prominent.

Her waist was as small as if she had whalebone stays built in instead of ribs, and her hips swelled quite fetchingly beneath that tiny waist span. She was a trifle long-waisted, though, her legs shapely but just the least bit short for her height.

She had delicate feet. And possibly the longest toes Longarm had ever seen on any human creature, though there'd been a hawk or eagle now and then with longer talons. Maybe.

It was her mouth, though, that interested him right at the moment.

And what she was wanting to do with it.

"Lie down, please," she whispered.

He sent a skeptical look around the small room. He sure as hell didn't recall seeing any beds nearby.

"On the table. It's all right. It's strong enough."

That sounded like the voice of experience, but it wasn't something a gentleman could ask a lady about. Longarm decided to take her word for it and did as she asked, kind of helped along by the fact that the girl was kissing him and guiding him in the direction she wanted him to go while already busy with the necessary buttons and buckles of his clothes.

He let her put him onto his back on the table—she was right, it was plenty strong enough—and failed to object while she sucked on his tongue and finished unbuttoning his britches.

"Oh, my," she whispered when she felt what was behind that open fly. "I knew you were handsome, dear. I didn't know you're hung like a stud horse besides." She laughed. "It just goes to show the rewards a girl can get for clean living and a charitable heart."

"Is that what this is?"

"Close enough, don't you think?"

"Close enough for my purposes, that's for sure."

"Now be quiet, dear, and let me enjoy what I've uncovered here."

Longarm resolved himself to silence.

Lucy lifted his hips and tugged his trousers out from under him, then spread his shirt and rolled him from side to side so she could get that off him too.

Once he was naked she clapped her hands with delight and chortled softly, a low and furry sound that was damn-all close to being the same sort of noise a cat makes when it goes to purring.

"Oh, my," she repeated. "Oh, this is lovely." Standing beside the table, she ran her hands over his chest, then bent and began to lick his nipples, both of which had become extremely sensitive to her touch.

Her tongue rambled slowly south, ranging down across his stomach and into his navel, then down again across his belly and into the mat of dark, curling hairs that lay at the base of his now pulsing shaft.

Lucy pulled back for a moment to admire the hard, glistening spear that was his manhood. She smiled and said, "Marvelous. I love it when they bump and bounce like that, all strong and hard and ready."

"Any time you want—"

"Hush now. We don't want to rush this, do we?"

"Uh, no, I reckon we don't at that."

"I'm so glad you agree with me, dear."

Longarm grinned. And mustered up a bit more patience. The girl seemed to be enjoying herself. It simply wouldn't be gentlemanly to take any of that away from her, would it?

"Lovely," she murmured. "Simply lovely." She leaned close over him so that he could feel her warm breath on the head of his cock. So close he was sure he could feel the warmth of her body reaching him. Yet without touching him. Quite. His pecker was so hard and ready now that it was bumping up and down with each and every heartbeat. If she didn't pretty damn soon . . .

The tip of her tongue flicked out. And again. Touching him lightly, ever so lightly. And each time that wet heat touched him his cock bounced up and away in unstoppable reaction. Lucy teased him over and over again, and laughed with the sheer pleasure of being the cause of his exquisite torment.

Just when Longarm decided he wasn't real sure he could take any more of that without grabbing the damn girl by the back of her head and ramming himself straight down her throat, she changed tactics.

This time she moved to the other side of his pecker and commenced lightly running her lips and tongue up and down the length of his shaft.

Longarm groaned a little and arched his pelvis upward in search of more.

Lucy giggled a little. And began to suck on his balls.

He cupped one breast in his hand and squeezed on it. "Harder," she whispered. He squeezed harder. "No, dear. Really hard. I mean it. As hard as you can manage."

It wasn't in him to do that, quite, but he did bear down plenty hard. Lucy shuddered, and he felt a ripple of—something—pain and pleasure alike, he thought, rush through her body.

With a moan she quit mouthing his scrotum and finally took the head of his cock into her mouth, sucking and pulling on him with her lips while her hands cupped his balls and encircled the base of his prick.

"Squeeze me again, dear. Harder. You won't hurt me, I promise. As hard as you can."

He bore down even harder on the flesh of her tit, and she groaned while she continued to suck and gobble.

He squeezed again and, shifting position so that she was poised above him, Lucy pushed her face down over him.

There was a moment of resistance as the head of his cock encountered the tight ring of cartilage at the entrance to her throat. Then she pushed through and beyond that point so that his shaft extended all the way inside her.

He could feel her chin pushing hard into his belly, and could feel the tip of her nose burrowing gently against his balls.

All in all the sensation was hellacious fine.

Gasping and panting for air, Lucy began to screw him with her throat, her lips a hot ring of flesh that was tight, tight around his cock and both her hands still busy teasing and stroking and tantalizing his cods.

She pulled away just far enough and just long enough to tell him, "It's all right, dear. You don't have to hold back. Go ahead and come in my mouth whenever you're ready. We'll get to the rest of it later."

That was sure as hell all the permission he needed. He'd been having trouble keeping himself from spewing his hot juice into her mouth since very shortly after she'd started in on him.

Now he stroked and caressed the back of her head and neck while she pushed herself fully onto him once more.

She took his hand and put it over her tit, squeezing his fingers as a reminder of what she wanted, and he bore down on her soft, pale flesh again, this time forgetting himself in the rush of pleasure she was giving him so that he damn near tore her breast clean off her chest.

He felt that swelling, demanding, insistent rush as the fluids boiled over beyond his ability to control, and his fist clamped with visc-like force on Lucy's breast while his juices gushed and jetted down her throat.

Lucy quivered and cried out in a climax of her own, the sounds of her squeal muffled by Longarm's pole, as the pleasure/pain in her tit sent her tumbling over the same precipice she'd just taken Longarm over.

Gasping then and sweating, she slowly withdrew, allowing his softening shaft to slip out of her throat and past her warm lips into the seemingly chill air of the very private little room.

"Damn," Longarm muttered.

Lucy smiled. "That, dear, is the very best dessert of all."

"Mighty glad to be of service, ma'am."

Her smile became a laugh. "Just so you don't think we're done."

"No?"

"Oh, my, no. There is still *so* much I want to do with you, Custis."

He lightly stroked her cheek, and she turned her head so that she could kiss his palm and run the tip of her tongue over it.

In spite of all that had just happened there was a stirring of desire that gathered low in his belly at the feel of her doing

45

that. Miss Lucy Watson, he thought, damn sure knew what she was doing.

Lordy, he sure reckoned that she did.

And there was no way he intended to leave this room before she'd done all she cared to do here.

"Y'know," he said, "I hadn't thought I'd wanted any dessert after that nice meal we had. Now I'm glad you talked me inta it."

Lucy threw her head back and laughed long and loud.

Chapter 9

Longarm stopped in the street and thumbed a match afire. He held the flame to the tip of his cheroot and got a healthy coal burning, then gratefully sucked the smoke deep into his lungs. He felt . . . empty. Drained. Hollow as a whore's heart. Lucy had pulled the juices out of him until there was nothing left. And then she'd taken more. Now he felt like there was a gaping void inside him from about his bellybutton down near to his knees. That kind of thinking was silly. He knew that. He felt it anyway.

Which is not to say he was complaining. Far from it. But it was a mildly disconcerting sensation to say the least, and now that he had it he wasn't real sure that he cared for it.

Still, if he had a chance to repeat the experience—and all that had led up to it—he reckoned he'd go right ahead and do it again.

Lordy, but that woman did know how to screw.

His cheroot glowing nicely and the taste of the smoke dry and bright in his mouth, Longarm ambled on down toward Emmaline Bertolucci's saloon. She'd said he should come back later to talk. Well, this was later and then some.

Unlike earlier in the afternoon, the place was plenty busy now. The corral held a dozen saddle horses or more, and there were seven or eight wagons parked outside. Behind the bar Gregory had an assistant. And damn well needed one. Obviously there was a good bit of foot traffic from the town as well as the customers who rode or drove in. The place was packed, the ceiling wreathed in blue-white smoke and the lamps adding their heat and smoke to the already fumy atmosphere caused by the heat and the stink of so many tightly packed bodies. Men were drinking, talking, pitching dice, and doing their damn-all best to cheat each other at cards. A few ugly tarts wearing dresses with skirts short enough and necklines low enough that no one would want to look at their pockmarked faces worked the room in search of low-rent loving. There was crowd enough that a man had to turn sideways or risk being elbowed in order to make his way through. Longarm breathed deep of the rank, smoky, smelly, perfumed stink. And smiled. He loved it.

"Rye whiskey?" Gregory asked when Longarm finally reached the bar.

Longarm shook his head. "Maybe later."

"You're really here on business?"

He nodded.

The barman sighed. And jerked his head to point his chin in the direction of the familiar doorway. "She's waiting for you."

Longarm paused before he moved in that direction. "Gregory?"

"Yeah?"

"I'll try an' not disappoint her. Or you."

A shadow as if from a cloud passing high overhead flitted briefly across the depths of Gregory's eyes. Then he nodded and turned back to his work. Longarm went behind the bar and through the door.

It was all Longarm could do to keep his expression from giving his feelings away. But he had to hide the truth. It would have been cruel to do otherwise.

Poor Emmy. Poor sad, stupid, used-up Emmy. She'd made an attempt to clean herself up since he'd been there earlier. She'd washed her face clean of all the caked crud and applied fresh makeup. She might as well not have bothered. The new application hadn't been laid on with a trowel. Hell, they didn't make trowels that big. The poor dumb broad must've used a shovel. There was powder and grease and bright color enough to paint a circus clown. The effect was bizarre and unsettling.

She'd changed to a fresh dress too, this one snowy white and bound tight at the waist, pushing her tits up and out so that they lay on top of the white satin bodice like a pair of hams on a shelf. Or, more like it, two lumps of suet on a rack.

The woman was grotesque. Longarm felt sorry for her. What she obviously wanted him to feel was desire. Poor, poor Emmy. There'd been a time . . .

"Hello, Emmy," he said gently.

"Custis." She smiled and simpered and fluttered her lashes enough to stir up a cyclone.

"You look mighty nice tonight, Emmy."

"You've never looked better yourself, Custis." She looked down suggestively toward a cushion beside her on the love seat where she'd chosen to present herself.

"I'd best not, Emmy. I came to talk, not . . . you know."

"I do know, Custis. How well I do remember." She sighed.

"So do I, Emmy. So do I." That, at least, was no lie.

"We could start over, Custis. You know how good me and you are together. Nobody's ever been like you, Custis. Nobody. Not even . . . not nobody."

"I'm sore tempted," he lied. "I remember every bit as good as you. But there's somebody in my life now, Emmy, and good a woman as you are, I know you wouldn't want me to be untrue. Not when I've made my pledge to her."

"You're married, Custis?"

"No, Emmy, not yet. I would've told you before if that was so. But we ain't real far from it. Time I've had my talk with Harry an' got back to Denver, I expect I'll be gettin' down onto a knee an' having a talk with *her*."

Emmaline closed her eyes and for a moment Longarm thought she was about to weep. But when she looked up again she managed a smile, a warm and true and genuine smile that was so fond and kind and selfless that Longarm felt like a real son of a bitch for having lied to her. "I wish you luck, Custis. Luck and happiness. I hope you know that."

"I was hopin' you would, Emmy."

"Nothing but, dear. Forever."

"You're a good woman, Emmy. An' a good friend."

Emmaline tilted her head to one side and looked at him for a moment. Then she grinned and shook her head.

"What?" he asked.

She only shook her head again.

"Aw, tell me. I could see you was thinking something. Tell me."

Emmy laughed. "I was wondering if this very lucky lady of yours has a father, Custis. Because I just realized that the thought of you having to ask some stern papa for your lady friend's hand is about the funniest thing I could ever think of."

Longarm chuckled too. "Y'know, Emmy, that's something I hadn't ever thought of my own self. Now that you mention it, it sure does sound scary."

"So, Custis. Does she have a father?"

"Yes, Emmy, she does have a father."

"Is he big, Custis? Does he have a mustache and scowl a lot?"

"Damn if I know, Emmy. I haven't met him yet. He's out in Idaho in a mining camp," Longarm said, glibly making up the yarn at the same time he spun it.

"What if he says no, Custis?"

"Emmy! Really! Who could say no to me?"

She laughed again. "Not me, dear. Never me. And I can't imagine anyone else refusing you either."

"You're a dear yourself, Emmy," he said, feeling much more comfortable now that Emmaline was no longer intent on trying to rekindle cold ashes. "Could we talk now?"

She sighed. And glanced this time toward a velvet-cushioned barrel chair nearby. "Sit down, Custis. I'll tell you everything I know about Harry. Including where he's working nowadays."

Chapter 10

To the great and overwhelming joy of such companies as the Denver and Rio Grande Railroad, Colorado Fuel and Iron, Estero Mining and Minerals, and Great Western Coal and Coke, the foothills of southern Colorado were riddled with easily accessible pockets of soft coal.

With railroads expanding rapidly throughout the entire West, and with the added needs of a burgeoning steel and foundry industry in nearby Pueblo—to say nothing of household heating and cooking needs—coal had quickly become a major factor in the mineral values of the state. Gold and silver were the headliners. But it was coal that was putting dividends into the pockets of investors, and in large measure too it was coal that was putting food onto the tables of the workingmen who laboriously dug it out of the ground. While relatively few men could handle the drilling and blasting that was required to extract gold ores, it took sweat and muscle, pick and pry bar—and plenty of manpower—to dig coal.

Fortunately for the needs of the state, there was a ready supply of coal available and of the men to dig it. Much of the Denver and Rio Grande right of way from the Arkansas River valley south all the way into New Mexico was paralleled by sharp-ridged foothills that held coal deposits lying conveniently close to the surface. The eastern slopes of the Wet Mountains and the Spanish Peaks were rotten with the stuff. And wherever coal was located, mines and towns grew ready to exploit the mineral wealth. The town of Cargyle was one of many such. Longarm had never been to Cargyle before. But he had certainly been to enough of its sisters to know what he could expect. A company town with company housing, company store, and company rules. The miners would take their wages from the company. And pay it all right back again for lodging, food, and whatever else a man might need. At Cargyle the company—if it mattered—was GWC&C, Great Western Coal and Coke. According to Emmaline Bertolucci, Harry Bolt was town marshal of Cargyle, which meant in essence that he was GWC&C's figurehead, hired man, and bullyboy. It would be Harry's job to keep the miners in line when they were above ground. The foremen and supervisors would ride herd on them the other twelve hours of each day.

Longarm roused to the call of the Denver and Rio Grande conductor and tipped his Stetson back away from his eyes. There was something about the racketing rattle-and-thump of a train in motion that ofttimes made him sleepy. He woke completely when the friendly conductor spoke to him, though, and reached for a cheroot, first offering one to the gent in the visored cap who'd been nice enough to warn him that his stop was ahead.

"Thanks," the conductor said. "Don't mind if I do."

"How long to Cargyle?" Longarm asked.

"You feel the train slowing?"

"Ayuh."

"That's for the stop at the Cargyle spur. Mind what I told you, though. There's no regular passenger traffic back into the hollow." Longarm guessed the conductor would be from Kentucky or possibly some other section in the heart of the Appalachians. Certainly not from the West, though, or he would have referred to the coal rich valley as a gulch, gully, or canyon. Only a mountain boy from somewhere in the South was likely to use the term hollow. "There might be some cuss with a cart come to see can he make a quarter, or you can tap into the wire and ask for someone to come fetch you in. One thing for damn sure, we ain't gonna stop and back all the way into Cargyle for the sake of one passenger even if he is a deputy marshal."

"I wouldn't ask you to do that anyhow," Longarm said. "You say it's only a mile or so?"

"Call it a mile and a half or something like it."

"Hell, that's no distance. I can walk that easier than having somebody come out an' get me."

The conductor gave him a look as if thinking Longarm might be slightly daft. But then in this country men weren't much for walking, not when they could find any sort of a ride.

"You do what you want, friend. Say, this is a mighty nice smoke. What brand did you say it is?"

Longarm told him and the man nodded sagely. Longarm did not mention the price. Probably the conductor would not have been quite so quick to nod if he knew that part of the deal. But then Longarm figured a man was entitled to treat himself to something special once in a while. After all, if he wasn't worth it, who the hell was?

The train rocked and shuddered as the speed fell off and the imperfections in the rail joints became all the more noticeable. Up ahead the engineer gave a long blast on the steam whistle.

"I asked Jules to let one go for you. It's possible somebody back in the hollow might hear and bring a wagon out for you."

"That's nice of you, friend. An' twice I owe you."

The conductor gave his cheroot an admiring look and winked. Longarm took the hint and gave the man a couple more of the slim, dark cigars to slip into his pocket for later.

Five minutes more and Longarm was standing alone on the gravel ballast—there wasn't even a platform for the use of main line passengers disembarking for Cargyle—beside a sign reading: CARGYLE, COLO, ELEVATION 4,216 FT. Underneath the painted lettering a wag had used something, probably a scrap of soft coal, to scrawl an addition: POPULATION ONE TOO DAMN MANY. Longarm wondered what the unhappy fellow had meant by that. That he didn't want to be there himself? Or that someone he didn't like was there? It could've been either one, Longarm figured as he drew in the last drag on his smoke and tossed the butt to the ground.

Standing there wasn't going to get him very far. He picked up his gear and commenced walking.

Like so many of these coal camps, like Ludlow a few miles south or Collier about eight miles north, Cargyle was in no way scenic.

There was dry bunchgrass prairie and a set of lonesome railroad tracks leading across it to disappear between two fingers of loose rock, the hillsides studded with dark green cedar and, here and there, a little scrub oak and low, spreading juniper. A creek bed, dry now and likely dry most of each year, ran along beside the tracks, as did a wagon road that didn't appear to see much use.

Longarm was about a quarter mile along the road and just about to get warmed up to the hike when he saw a pale curl of dust rising near the entrance to the canyon—or hollow, if one preferred—where the tracks led.

The dust became more and more clearly visible, and soon a buckboard came into view. The wagon was fair flying along. And close behind it a two-wheeled cart bounced crazily, only one wheel at a time touching the earth as the pony between the bars raced to get ahead of the team of cobs that were pulling the buckboard.

The two vehicles seemed an unlikely match for a race, but the price of the entertainment was certainly right, so Longarm paused in his walking so he could enjoy the contest.

Wagon and cart careened closer, the driver of the wagon several times deliberately veering in front of the cart to force the red and white pony into the creek bed. The driver of the paint had to either give way or crash. He chose to give way, but he didn't much like it. As the racing vehicles came ever nearer, Longarm could hear the drivers swearing at each other. They were shouting and hollering about as hard as they were driving. Neither one of them was much more than a kid, Longarm saw once they were close enough. He guessed the wagon driver to be about fourteen, the boy in the cart a year or two younger.

Both of them were dashing hellbent, urging their animals, screaming insults, leaning forward and straining as if that would somehow lend speed to their rigs. The wagon and the cart alike were bouncing high into the air and wobbling from side to side so hard it was an amazement that either boy could remain inside his own vehicle, much less keep any degree of control.

Longarm was so busy watching all this with a sense of detached amusement that it damn near failed to dawn on him that he was standing in the very same road these boys were racing down.

Once the realization finally dawned, he had to step lively to reach the safety of the railroad tracks in time to avoid being run over.

He escaped with his life, if not with quite all his dignity, and turned to see, much to his surprise, both boys setting back hard on their driving lines and struggling to turn their excited animals around. Horses and pony alike were fighting the bits and wanting to race on.

"Whoa, you sons of bitches, whoa," the older boy in the wagon was shouting.

"Me, mister, pick me," the younger one shrieked, cutting straight to the heart of the matter and seeking to claim a prize he hadn't exactly won.

Longarm reckoned he had to thank that conductor fella all over again for being thoughtful enough to ask for a toot on the train whistle.

It seemed that his transportation into Cargyle had arrived.

Chapter 11

The boys were named Buddy and Rick. Buddy was the younger one with the pony and cart. Rick was the kid with the buckboard. In, about, and through all the yammering, the cussing—some of it fairly inventive considering the early ages of the cussers—and the accusations, Longarm worked it out that Buddy had a mother who was the legitimate owner of the pony and cart rig and that Rick was a sometime employee of the greengrocer who was the true owner of the wagon and team. There was some question, at least in Buddy's mind, as to whether Rick was officially authorized to utilize the buckboard for purposes of secondary employment. This was not a question Longarm felt qualified to arbitrate, so he settled the matter short of fisticuffs by offering a compromise solution.

"What I'm gonna do," he told the red-faced and furious combatants, "is hire the both of you. Rick, I'm gonna pay you a dime, hard money, to carry my bag an' saddle in that wagon there. An' Buddy, I'm gonna pay you a dime to carry me on the seat of that cart. Buddy, don't you dare open that mouth of yours till I'm finished talking; d'you think I don't see your lip floppin' open? You hush up too there, Rick. Now . . . *if* I c'n finish what I was fixin' to say here . . . the deal is this. We'll do 'er just like I said or else I'll walk the rest of the way like

I started out to do to begin with. So you each do like I say an' work together so's each of you makes hisself a dime . . . or else you don't neither one earn a damn thing. Suit yourselves."

There was no discussion necessary and scant hesitation. Rick jumped down off the buckboard to grab Longarm's things and stow them carefully into the wagon bed, while Buddy was just as quick to steady his pony, still agitated and wanting to run after the excitement of the race, so the paying customer could climb onto the cart.

A couple minutes more and they were moving calmly— well, more or less so—in the direction of Cargyle.

The town pretty much turned out to be a repeat of all the other coal mining company towns along this stretch of country.

At the mouth of the shallow canyon leading into Cargyle a meager scattering of shanties, saloons, and businesses of dubious purpose sat like a clump of toadstools between the railroad tracks and the creek bed. These, Longarm knew, would be the few genuine private businesses to be found hereabouts. Some of them anyhow. Many of the big companies owned these "shadow" businesses that popped up wherever there were workingmen drawing regular pay. And for sure, regardless of who might actually own the places, none could operate here without the consent of the all-powerful company, in Cargyle's case the GWC&C. All of them, however, would be situated on public land, or at least on parcels that were not directly owned by the company. That pattern seemed to be inviolable because with it the company could not be blamed for anything unsavory that might take place close to, but not located directly upon, company property.

In this particular instance there wasn't any signpost or gate to show where the company property line was drawn. But Longarm could guess at it close enough for his purposes. It would be within twenty feet, maybe less, of the last shanty in this clump of pathetic businesses. Everything beyond that would belong to Great Western Coal and Coke.

As for what all of that might encompass, he couldn't yet actually see. But once again he knew good and well what to expect, at least in a generalized sort of way.

From the mouth of the canyon he could see the creek bed, the rails, and the winding, dusty roadway. Beyond that, somewhere past the first bend in the irregular hillsides, several plumes of pale smoke lifted into the midday air. Up there he knew he would find dozens and dozens of tiny box-like shacks that would be the company housing rented out to men with wives and children. There would be barracks-like boardinghouses, huge and efficient chow halls, fairly grand administrative offices, and some nice homes that would be assigned to the company managers, a company store or possibly several of them, one of which would include a post office, a small jail—and dominating everything else, above and beyond all the rest of it, there would be the coal. Gaping drift mouths with the black residues spreading fan-like beneath the openings. Great storage piles and railcar loading hoppers. Steam engines to drive the conveyors. Tool sheds and handcars and all the thousand and one things it took to make a mine and keep it functioning.

Cargyle, Longarm knew, had nothing to do with structures and damn little to do with people. What Cargyle was, had been, and always would be was *coal*. And nothing but.

"You goin' up to the offices, mister?" little Buddy asked.

"I don't know, son. Is there a hotel up there?"

"No hotel here, mister. No need for one. Everybody that comes here gets company housing one way or another. If he don't get company housing, then he ain't welcome anyhow and might as well go back where he come from."

Longarm suspected the kid was quoting most of that speech. But the message was clear enough anyway. He scratched under his chin and pondered. He wasn't at all sure he would qualify to be given a room courtesy of the GWC&C. And if he did

60

qualify, he wasn't at all sure that he'd want one. Not that he had anything against the GWC&C. He didn't. But he sure as hell wouldn't want to be beholden to Harry Bolt. Not in any way, shape, or form.

"I tell you what, son. Let's see if we can find any place out here where I might put up for a night or two. I, uh, I'd pay for the lodging, of course. Can you think of anybody that'd—"

"My ma would let you stay with us, mister. You could have my bed an' I can make up a place on the floor. It wouldn't cost you much. And my ma cooks real good. Honest. You'll see."

Rick, sitting on the spring seat of the buckboard nearby, sneered and in a nasty tone of voice said, "His ma is a whore, mister. Give her fifty cents an' she'll lick your dingus till you pee in her mouth."

Longarm reached out in time to snag Buddy by the back of his britches and haul him back onto the seat of the cart. The much smaller boy had launched himself at Rick before all the words were even out of the older kid's mouth. "That's a lie, you dirty sonuvabitch, stinking bastard, yellow shitface dog screwer."

Longarm admired the intensity of the emotion, but didn't figure he could award Buddy very many points for class or imagery. "Whoa, dammit," he ordered loudly. "Rick, I want you to apologize to Buddy."

"But . . ."

"No buts, dammit. Even if you believe what you said is true—and mind, I'm not no way claiming that it is—but even if you believe it, Rick, it's an ugly thing for anybody to say. A person has dignity and pride. I'm sure you want Buddy to respect yours, so you gotta show him you're willing to respect his. So I want you to take back what you just said." Longarm gave the older boy a hooded look, which got the kid's attention.

"Yes, sir. I'm sorry."

"Don't say it to me, son, say it to Buddy."

"Buddy, I'm sorry I said bad things about your ma."

"All right. Buddy, tell Rick you accept his apology."

"But . . ."

"Do it!"

"Yessir. Rick, I . . . you know. What he said."

"Tell him," Longarm said.

Buddy sighed. "I accept you apologizing. An' my ma ain't no hoor."

"I already said she wasn't."

"No, you said you was sorry you said she was. You never said that she wasn't."

"All right then, I say she ain't. Is that better?"

"Yeah. That's better."

Longarm let go of his hold on Buddy's britches and climbed down off the cart. "If we're all done venting our spleens, boys, let's see if I can hire that bed for tonight. You run on ahead an' check on that, Buddy. Rick and me will bring my things along."

Buddy hadn't any more than gotten out of earshot than Rick put on another sneer and a swagger and said, "His ma really is a whore, mister. I know that for a fact. For a dollar she'll . . ."

Longarm shut him up with a hard look, and this time the kid had sense enough to stay shut up.

Chapter 12

Longarm walked from the property line to the administration buildings of Cargyle. It was further than he'd expected, and he was glad he didn't have to lug his gear all that way.

He'd passed row after row of tiny, pillbox houses, all of them with clotheslines strung outside and most of them with toys littering the front stoops as well. There was no sign of the barracks that would be provided for the single men. Apparently GWC&C kept them separate.

There was the expected company store and a rickety-looking school building—empty at this hour when from every side he could smell the scents of evening meals being prepared—and deep inside the narrow, winding canyon he finally caught sight of the complex of handsomely built native-stone structures that would be the GWC&C offices.

A flagpole stood before the biggest of the administration buildings, but no flag flew from it.

In the distance to the west, walled in on north and south alike by the nearly barren slopes of the foothill ridges, he could see the first of the ironwork skeletons that marked the actual mining operations. Between those loading hoppers and the administration buildings were the single-story barracks where the bachelors would be housed. Large mess halls added their smoke and smells to the evening, but the food scents at this end of the company town were not nearly as tantalizing as those he'd smelled back among the family quarters.

Immediately beyond the administration buildings and conveniently close to the single miners' barracks was a stone structure about ten by twenty feet in size and with iron bars covering the one window Longarm could see. Closer inspection confirmed the obvious. A sign over the door read: CARGYLE JAIL. The door stood open, and Longarm stepped inside without knocking.

The jail had been divided into three sections, each of more or less equal size. The middle was an office holding a desk, two chairs, and a small table. Either end of the place had been walled off with metal bars. Each cell held a steel cot. Period. No other provision had been made for the prisoners' comfort. There was no thunder mug, no water jar, and no mattress or blankets on the cots. A lone window at either end of the building lent a bit of light and air . . . and in winter no doubt admitted a great deal of discomfort as well since there were no shutters or other means to cover the unglazed openings. Wind, rain, and snow were as free to enter as the air. Perhaps because of that, no heating stove had been installed, although a framework had been built into the ceiling where a stovepipe could be accommodated.

The central-office portion of the small building was empty, but the cell to the right of the door held a thin fellow with black grime trapped as if permanently in the wrinkles of his skin and under his fingernails. He had lank once-blond hair and a pleasant grin.

"H'lo there. Be a chum, will you? Look in that desk, bottom left drawer, and hand me my box. It's my chewing t'baccy I need out of it, that's all. Go on now. You'll see it. It's the only box in there, a little thing about so big"—he motioned with his hands to indicate something about the size of a cigar box—

"with the stuff from my pockets in it. Go on, chum. Nobody will mind."

"Sorry," Longarm said. "I'm just here looking for Harry Bolt."

"Lucky you, eh? Or maybe you don't know our Harry." The prisoner laughed. "In that case lucky you, but this time I mean it, right?"

"Just tell me where I can find him, please."

"First the box, chum. Then we'll talk."

"No, first you answer a civil question."

"Screw you."

Longarm shrugged, glanced once around the place again to make sure he hadn't overlooked anyone or anything that might be helpful, then started back outside.

"Hey!" the prisoner howled. "You can't just leave me here."

"Watch me," Longarm said.

"Then at least tell those bastards that I'm getting plenty damn hungry in here and I'm thirsty and I gotta take a shit."

Longarm went back to the main administration building, the one with the flagpole out front, and mounted the steps to a broad veranda that stretched across the full width of the building front. Several tidy groupings of rocking chairs had been set out in pairs, each pair placed so they flanked low drink tables that had checkerboards inlaid into the tabletops in contrasting shades of wood. The chairs and the tables looked like none of them had ever been used. But they were decorative. He supposed that was what they were there for, so they were accomplishing their purpose.

"Can I help you?" a pale gent in sleeve garters asked from behind a low counter when Longarm came inside.

"I'm looking for Harry Bolt, friend. I'm told he's town marshal here."

"Chief of police, actually. We prefer that title."

"Whatever. Point is, where is he?"

The little fellow with the crisp, unblemished collar—Longarm would've bet half a month's pay, maybe more, on the belief that this young yahoo drew his pay from the Great Western Coal and Coke company but hadn't ever yet set foot underground in one of those filthy old coal mines, and furthermore wasn't damn well likely to in the future—smiled oh-so-politely and asked, "And just what business is it of yours, may I ask?"

Longarm smiled back just as politely—and every bit as insincerely—and dragged out his wallet to show the badge.

"Deputy United States . . . um, you say you are looking for our Chief Bolt, Marshal?"

"Official business," Longarm said. "But don't get your bowels in no uproar. It ain't anything to do with the company. Has to do with a federal matter outa Wyoming that Chief Bolt may be able to help us with." Well, that was more or less true so far as it went. The GWC&C clerk wasn't entitled to all the details, not the way Longarm saw it.

"Chief Bolt is away for the rest of the day, Marshal. He mentioned earlier that he was going down to Ludlow to see Chief Wilcox about something—I have no idea what—and I believe the two of them planned to go on down to Trinidad for the evening. I suggest you look for him in the morning. Unless your business is urgent, of course. In that case you might think about going back out to the main line and flagging the nine o'clock southbound."

Longarm grunted and thanked the man. He didn't reckon there was any need to chase Bolt all the way down to Trinidad, though—where, dammit, he'd just been a few hours earlier—because if Longarm couldn't find Harry here, then neither could young Steve Reese. Morning should be quite good enough.

Longarm muttered a perfunctory good-bye and went back to where Rick was waiting to take him to the shack where the boy named Buddy had said he could take lodging for the night.

Chapter 13

Buddy's mother turned out to be a thin, rather plain woman of thirty or so. When Longarm got there she was cooking supper, which turned out to be a rice concoction laced heavily with chunks of onion and squash and containing a few pale shreds of something that might have been chicken. Or maybe something else that Longarm would just as soon not identify anyway. But at least the meal was cheap. It was also, he would soon discover, tastier than he'd expected. The woman knew how to use spices to perk up an otherwise bland and dreary diet.

Her name was Angela. She wiped her hands carefully on her apron before she offered her hand to Longarm in greeting. "Eric has been telling me about you, Mr. Long."

"Eric," Longarm repeated. "I take it that'd be the young fella there?" He hooked a thumb in Buddy's direction and gave the kid a grin.

Angela Fulton smiled. "I'm his mother. I can get away with calling him by his real name. But I suspect if you try it, Mr. Long, you're apt to get a kick in the shins for your trouble."

"Then I reckon I'd best leave off, hadn't I."

"Let me take your hat, Mr. Long. And sit, please. At the

table would be fine. You, uh . . . Eric tells me that you would be willing to pay for lodging?"

"That's right, ma'am."

"Would fifty cents be too much?"

"Oh, I dunno, ma'am. I was thinking it oughta be more like a dollar."

"I'm a poor negotiator, Mr. Long, so I suppose I shall just have to give in and accept your terms."

"I'm right glad you're so easy to get along with, Mrs. Fulton."

"Eric, have you washed your hands ready for supper?"

"No, Ma."

"Then take Mr. Long with you and show him where the basin is. And mind you let him use the towel first. Lord only knows what manner of things you'll leave behind even if you do remember to use the soap this time."

Buddy grinned and motioned for Longarm to follow him outside.

Longarm washed first, then the kid, Buddy talking nonstop the whole while. When they were done Longarm emptied the basin and refilled the water pail from a rain barrel at the corner of the shanty. The water level was getting low and pretty soon someone—Buddy came to mind—was going to have to fill it again, presumably with creek water since this was not the rainy season and there didn't appear to be a well close by.

"Does your mama mind a gentleman smoking indoors?" Longarm asked, thinking ahead to after dinner.

"No. My pa used to smoke. I think. Anyhow you can go ahead. She won't mind."

"Thanks." That was the first anyone had mentioned the missing Mr. Fulton. Longarm wondered what had become of him, but didn't want to come right out and ask in case the answer would bring back hurtful memories for Buddy and his mother.

Supper did prove to be both tasty and filling, and Longarm had no complaint about the quality of the board to be gained for his dollar. Or more accurately, for the government's dollar, as he would put this down on a voucher for Billy Vail's clerk Henry to quibble and quarrel over but eventually pay.

When, after the meal, he reached inside his coat for a cheroot, Mrs. Fulton brought him an ashtray and a candle to light his cigar from. He crossed his legs and settled back in some contentment.

"Eric James, you can do the washing up this evening, and if Mr. Long wants more coffee you can pour it for him. I have to go out for a little while."

The boy's face fell. Longarm assumed Buddy was embarrassed about having to do the dishes with a stranger looking on. Instead, though, he said, "Can't you stay home tonight, Ma? Please?"

"Hush, Eric. You know I have to work."

"But Ma . . ."

"Hush, I said." She looked at Longarm and explained, "I have an evening job at the laundry and dry cleaning up in Cargyle. Eric always resents being alone at night for some reason."

Longarm knew what that reason was, of course, but he wasn't fixing to mention it. He had to wonder, though, about the rumor that boy Rick was spreading. Something like that could sure as hell hurt a lady's reputation for it always seems to be the ugliest rumors that spread the quickest and take the deepest roots.

Angela Fulton gathered up a light shawl to put over her shoulders against the chill of the evening, then said her good-byes. Longarm stood to watch her out of the house, then sat back down again to finish his cheroot while Buddy turned to the chore of cleaning up the dishes and wiping down the table. To his credit the kid didn't skimp on the job and didn't try to put it off either.

Nor, Longarm noticed, did he resume the lighthearted talkativeness that he'd been given to earlier. Back, Longarm realized, when he'd thought the income from this overnight guest would keep his ma from having to go out and work tonight.

Once his smoke was done Longarm stretched and contemplated the remainder of an evening that was still very young. The sun was barely down, and all he had to look forward to now was the dubious comfort to be found on the stretched canvas cot where Buddy normally slept.

"I tell you what, son."

"Yes, sir?"

"You don't need me around here, and I'm sure not sleepy enough yet to be wanting to go to bed. I think I'll wander down the way an' see can I find a card game to sit in on."

"Oh, I don't think there's any gambling allowed around here, mister. I'm pretty sure it's again' the law."

"If I can't find a game then, Buddy, I'll settle for a drink and a little conversation. You aren't scared of being alone here, are you?"

"No, sir."

"All right then. You tend to things here. And don't worry. I won't be out late, and when I come in I'll be real quiet in case you're asleep."

"I won't be asleep, mister." The boy looked upset, although Longarm didn't know what he had to be concerned with.

Longarm retrieved his hat from the wall hook where Mrs. Fulton had left it. With a wink and a cheerful word to Buddy, Longarm went out into the cool night air that swept down through the Cargyle canyon to spill out onto the grassy flats that began here at the canyon mouth.

Chapter 14

The saloon—it was the biggest and most popular of the several that were available at this unofficial end of Cargyle—was so cheap and basic that they didn't stock any form of rye whiskey, much less the excellent Maryland distilled rye that was Longarm's preference. They had bar whiskey—Lord only knows what might be found in it in addition to bulk alcohol; tobacco, red peppers, and gunpowder were common ingredients—at twelve and a half cents or bottled bourbon at fifteen cents. Longarm took a look at the stained and faded labels on the bourbon bottles and suspected the only difference between the bourbon and the bar whiskey here would turn out to be the price. He settled for beer, and strolled to the side of the room where, Buddy's cautions apart, there was some gaming in progress.

It took Longarm little more than a glance to decide that these were not friendly games among gents who were whiling the hours away. These were serious attempts by poor workingmen to wrest gaudy sums of cash from the house.

Wherever one can find a deck of cards, a pair of dice, or a wheel of fortune one can also find hope. Longarm understood that. What he also understood, and these soot-stained miners obviously did not, was that generally speaking a gambling house doesn't take any gambles when it opens a game for play.

In all games the edge belongs to the house. Hell, that's what all the rules are *for,* to ensure that basic truth.

Some houses are greedier than others, but there really isn't any need for any of them to rig their wheels or load their dice. An edge belonging to the house is built right into the play. The house will just naturally win, even at poker, where a genuinely honest game can be played whenever the house is willing to take a rake off the ante of each hand and leave everything else to the relative skills of the players. That, Longarm knew, was the fairest and most honest play available in any casino or gaming hall.

Still, some folks can't be content with winning a constant percentage. They want to take it all.

And judging from what he could see here, whoever ran this place wanted it all.

Within ten minutes of standing there sipping at his beer Longarm could spot three shills who were working for the place. They were easy to locate. They were the ones that were winning.

And of course every time one of them won, there was a loud huzzah as onlookers cheered and hangers-on crowded close so they too could play at the "hot" tables where all this winning was taking place.

The whole thing was damn near funny because the shills were so blatant they didn't even pretend to be workingmen themselves. They dressed in rough clothes and clophopper brogans, but their fingernails were clean and the backs of their necks had seen neither coal dust nor bright sun in many a year.

And these boys won no matter what games they played. Roulette, the wheel of fortune, craps, faro, or poker, it didn't matter. They'd lose a little, then win a lot. And every time one of them won it spurred the suckers—the real players—on to fresh enthusiasm.

Longarm was tempted to sit in on one of the games just so he could have the pleasure of exposing the sham. It wouldn't be hard to do. Find the wire, the magnet, the birdshot, the marks . . . whatever. Lay it out for all to see and raise some hell.

But dammit, cheating at cards wasn't exactly a federal offense, and personal satisfaction wasn't what Longarm had come here to find.

The sensible thing for him to do, he knew, was to go quietly away. Get a good night's sleep and maybe talk about this place when he saw Harry Bolt in the morning.

After all, this was Harry's town, not his. And Longarm had good reason to know how touchy Harry Bolt could get. Pissing Harry off before he ever said howdy probably wasn't a tactic Billy Vail would approve.

So Longarm kept his mouth shut and his cash in his pocket. He reckoned he'd finish this beer and go back to the Fulton house. If nothing else, maybe they'd have something there that he could read until he got sleepy enough to head for the blankets. He manufactured a yawn in an attempt to encourage a drowsy state of mind, and took another look around the crowded barroom.

He looked. And then looked hard yet again.

There was something about one of the bar girls that . . . aw, shit, he told himself.

The woman caught his eye as he was staring at her. Beneath the white powder and bright red rouge she paled and gasped for breath.

After a moment's hesitation she started across the floor to where Longarm stood gaping at her.

Chapter 15

"Evenin', Miz Fulton." Longarm tipped his Stetson to the, um, lady. He wasn't sure, but underneath all the powder and gunk on her face he thought he could detect a flush of crimson embarrassment.

"Good evening, Mr. Long. Would you mind not calling me by my name, though? Not here. My working name is Dovie."

"Dovie?" He smiled. And again thought he could see that hint of blush beneath all the war paint.

"You don't have to make fun of me, Mr. Long. I don't particularly want everyone to know who I am, those that don't already. And anyway, the gents like names like Dovie and Frenchie and Lily LaTour. Those are really good names for whores."

He sobered. "I'm sorry, Miz . . . I mean, Dovie. I'm not making fun. Truly, I ain't." He looked around. And smiled just a little. "Though I can't see much in the way of gents in here for anybody to impress." The room was crowded. But definitely not with gentlemen.

Angela Fulton, though, was not thinking in terms of light banter. Not at this moment. She touched his sleeve and there was something in her eyes—a sadness, a loneliness—that also touched his heart. "When you go back tonight . . ."

"I won't say nothing to Buddy." His smile was gentle and sincere. "After all, there's nothing to tell, is there?"

"No. Of course not." She looked like she was on the brink of tears, and when she turned away from him her gait was slow and unhappy.

"Dovie." He called her back before the thought was consciously formed in his mind.

"Yes?"

"I was thinkin' . . . how much would it be for you to come with me?"

She lifted her chin and her expression firmed. The look in her eyes now was harder, colder. She was, he was sure, steeling herself against the hand fate had dealt. "A dollar, Mr. Long. Fifty cents for a stand-up in the alley or the dollar if you want the use of a bed. But don't worry. I won't insist that you take your boots off."

He refused to let her subtle needling reach him. "That'd be for a quickie. What I had in mind was all night."

"Normally I would charge five dollars for the full night, Mr. Long. But for you, considering that I already provided a bed we can use, I think ten dollars would be appropriate."

Obviously she was thinking he wanted to take her back to her house and go at it with her son right there close enough to hear their bellies bump.

"Ten dollars would be fine," Longarm said and, sweeping his hat off, bowed her toward the door.

"You can't be serious."

"Ten dollars you asked and ten dollars it shall be, ma'am." He pulled his money out and handed her a gold eagle, the same approximate size of a silver dime but worth ten dollars. "That should cover it, right?"

She gave him a hateful look. But took the money.

Silently she led the way out into the cool night air. Longarm waited until they were outside where none of the saloon patrons could overhear, then said, "Shouldn't you wash your face an' get your own dress back before we go to the house, Miz Fulton?"

She glared at him. But considered. And finally nodded.

"I'll wait for you here," he suggested. "Join me on the corner when you're ready, an' I'll walk you home."

"Very well." Without another look in his direction Angela Fulton disappeared into the mouth of the alley that ran between the saloon and its next-door neighbor.

Longarm idled over to the street corner where he'd said he would meet Buddy's mother. He leaned against a lamppost and pulled out a cheroot, taking his time about trimming the twist and forming a damn-near-perfect coal for his smoke.

Men came and went along the beaten-earth path that served this part of Cargyle in the place of a normal board sidewalk. Longarm recognized none of them. That was hardly surprising since he'd never been here before. But then checking over a crowd for faces he'd seen on wanted posters was something that had become a firmly entrenched habit with him, and for that matter with every other good peace officer he'd ever known. It was something a man did practically without conscious thought.

Mrs. Fulton did not need long to change. Longarm hadn't finished half his cigar before she emerged from the side of the saloon building and came into the circle of light thrown by the oil lamp Longarm was standing under. Her face was scrubbed clean now and the dress beneath her shawl was drab and shapeless. The painted chippy named Dovie had disappeared as completely as if she'd never existed, leaving plain and dowdy Angela Fulton behind.

"That looks better," Longarm said, once again tipping his hat to her. "Shall we—"

His invitation was interrupted by a voice from the doorway of the saloon.

"Dovie!"

Mrs. Fulton jumped as if she'd been slapped. Longarm turned to see who it was who'd spoken.

The man standing in the door frame was a burly fellow of middle age. He was balding on top, but balanced that with a handlebar mustache of monumental proportions. His arm and shoulder muscles bulged practically beyond the limits of mere clothing to contain, and he looked like he could lift full beer barrels and smash them open on his own noggin without ever raising a sweat. Longarm had seen him inside seated at a table off to one side of the busy room, but hadn't paid particular attention to him then. After all, the man's appearance didn't match that of any known felon or suspect that Longarm was aware of.

"Yes, Clete?" Which answered *that* question anyway. Longarm might not know the fellow, but Mrs. Fulton certainly did.

"You changed clothes."

"Yes, Clete."

"Don't you think you aren't working the rest of tonight, bitch. And don't you *ever* think you can go off without giving me my share. Try that, bitch, and I'll beat you to a bloody pulp. You know I'd do it too, don't you, bitch?"

"Yes, Clete. I know you'll do what you say. I know you would." Angela squeezed her eyes tightly shut for a moment, then stared down at the ground once she reopened them. She seemed not to want to look at Longarm.

For his part, Clete seemed to be enjoying showing off in front of this stranger. Longarm suspected he was one of those men who like to keep a woman in line by smacking her around and proving to her just how much power he holds over her. But then, hell, the bitches are only women, right? And women all need a little smacking around now and then.

Clete strutted a step or two forward and, to emphasize his warning, pulled a heavy clasp knife out of his pocket and with a flick of his wrist snapped it open. The blade had a locking arrangement on it so that once opened it was as sturdy as a skinning knife. And as deadly.

Angela took a look at the blade shining in the lamplight. She shuddered and bit her lower lip.

Longarm drifted a bit forward and to his left, putting himself between Clete and Angela as casually as if he hadn't noticed it happening. He yawned and reached into his pocket. "I haven't paid the lady yet, Clete. Whyn't I make this easy on everybody an' just give you the money. Then you can hand over her split later."

"Now that sounds fine to me, fella," Clete said. "You agreeable to that, bitch?"

"Yes, Clete. Whatever you say." Mrs. Fulton's voice was timid, and Longarm could hear a tremor of fear in it.

"Pay it over then, mister."

"Five dollars was the piece we agreed on," Longarm said. "Does that sound right?"

"Five for a piece of that stupid bitch's miserable ass? Mister, I don't know where you come from, but I'd sure as hell like to run a stable of girls there."

"The five was to be for all night," Longarm explained patiently.

"Shit, you're probably still being overcharged. But yeah, that sounds better. So okay, mister. Hand it over and get the bitch outa my sight."

Longarm smiled and counted five dollars in change into the man's palm. "We're straight now, right?"

"Yeah. Right," Clete grunted, dropping the coins into his pocket.

"I just wanted to be sure." His smile was lazy now. Slow and easy. And stopping short of reaching his eyes. "The little lady's out of it now, right?"

"Yeah, sure, buddy. Whatever."

"Good. Mind if I take a look at that?" Without waiting for an answer, Longarm reached out and gently extracted the lockblade from the big man's fingers.

"Hey! What the hell do you think you're . . ."

With no attempt to answer, and still smiling, Longarm bent over to place the knife point-down in the soil, leaning the handle against the base of the lamppost.

"What the . . ."

One quick jab with the heel of Longarm's boot and the lockblade broke in half at the hinge, the now useless blade driving partway into the ground and the empty handle skittering away in the dirt.

"You son of a bitch!"

Clete had barely started forward when Longarm spun, the momentum of his turn and the weight of his body adding impetus to the wicked left that hooked forearm-deep into Clete's belly.

Clete cried out, his voice amazingly high-pitched and squeaky, and doubled over gasping for breath.

"It's something a man oughta remember," Longarm suggested in a deceptively soft tone of voice. "When you pull a knife in front of another man, Clete, it's a real good idea to think ahead of time about how he's gonna take it. You know?"

Clete still couldn't breathe. He dropped to his knees, sucking air and clutching his midsection.

"You ain't much of a man with a knife, Clete," Longarm continued. "Next time mayhap you oughta try with a gun." He grinned, the expression nonetheless cold and chilling. "If you feel real, *real* lucky." Longarm looked at the bullying whoremaster a moment longer. Then turned and walked away. If he heard the oily snick of a pistol hammer being cocked . . .

But there was no such threat.

Not from Clete. Not when it was a grown man instead of some poor, cowering little whore to be faced.

Longarm walked away and left Angela Fulton to catch up in her own good time.

Chapter 16

"It's time for you to go to bed now, son."

"But Ma, it's only—"

"Eric!" The sharpness in her voice was as cutting as the lash on a bullwhip.

"Yes, Ma." The boy gave Longarm a hangdog look. It was plain the kid felt he was being treated like a kid here and didn't like it. Not in front of a grown-up male guest in particular he didn't like it.

Longarm gave the boy a shrug and a quick roll of the eyes that Mrs. Fulton couldn't see. Aloud he told the kid, "You an' me both gotta do what your mama says, Buddy. But I got an idea."

"Yeah?"

"That bed o' yours is back there close to your mama's room. It wouldn't be right was I to bunk down over there. That's the sort of thing could set folks to talking an' we wouldn't want that. Whyn't you go on an' sleep in your own bed tonight like always. I'll stretch out on the pallet you've made by the stove here."

"But that wasn't the deal. I promised you a bed."

"An' a bed I'll have," Longarm said agreeably. He grinned and added, "Besides, my ol' feet won't hang over the end of

81

a pallet. With a regular-size cot I'm like to start fallin' off here an' there. Next thing you know it'll come morning an' I'll be all twisted up like one of them salty German baked dough things. What is it they call them doodads?"

"Pretzels," Buddy said.

"Yeah, pretzels, that's what I'd be come morning. We can't have that, can we?"

"You're sure about this, mister? Honest?"

"Honest," Longarm assured him.

Buddy glanced at his mother for her approval of the change in plan, and when she nodded he said his good nights.

"Don't let me sleep past breakfast, hear?" Longarm said.

"I won't," the kid promised. Never mind that anyone wanting to build a fire in the stove would have to step over whoever slept on the pallet on the floor. And that was ignoring too the fact that Longarm was a mighty light sleeper, as anyone in his particular line of work pretty much had to be.

Buddy stepped out of his britches and crawled into his cot. His mother gave Longarm a quizzical look—the gent had paid for her services several times over already and yet this was not going at all the way she'd expected—and went to tuck her son into bed. She pulled the covers high under his chin and gave him a kiss on the forehead, then unfolded a quilt and used it as a makeshift drape to separate Buddy's cot from the main room of the shanty. Her own "bedroom" was walled off, sort of, by muslin sheeting that had been tacked into place. The shack really was a one-room affair, but the makeshift dividers turned it into a tiny two-bedroom house.

Angela Fulton carefully arranged the quilt so Buddy could not see out, then gave Longarm a worried look and came slowly, almost shyly toward him.

Longarm faked a huge yawn and a stretch and said, plenty loud enough that he was sure Buddy could hear, "Reckon I'm gettin' a mite sleepy too, ma'am. If you don't mind, I'll step outside an' smoke one more cigar before I turn in. No need for you to wait up an' see me back inside, though. I'll bar the door when I come to bed."

"But Mr. Long . . . I . . . don't know what to say."

"G'night is the custom, ma'am." Longarm grinned. "But you say whatever it is you have in mind."

"I . . . good night, Mr. Long."

"Good night, Mrs. Fulton." He turned and went outside, a slim cheroot already in hand.

Longarm's eyes snapped open. He was instantly awake, not yet sure of what he'd heard or sensed to bring him out of his sleep, but certain there had been something, some noise or movement or inexplicable mental alarm, that roused him.

The shanty was dark as a tax collector's intentions save for a faint, scarcely discernible red glow from embers dying in the stove. The fact that a few coals were still pulsing heat and light meant he hadn't been sleeping for very long. Call it two hours tops and probably less, Longarm judged. His right hand slid surreptitiously toward the butt of the double-action Colt revolver he'd laid beside his head before sinking into sleep. If it was danger that was approaching . . .

The faint sounds of cloth rustling softly in the night drew his attention away from the door, the area most likely to present danger, and toward the back of the small house.

Longarm could hear Buddy's slow, monotonous breathing as the boy slept.

Which pretty much narrowed the possibilities.

He let go of his hold on the revolver and pushed gun and holster away.

Angela Fulton reached his side and dropped to her knees. There was enough light given off through the stove damper that he could make out the pale form that was her nightgown and the dim shape of her face and limbs.

Thinking only to let her know that he was already awake he touched her wrist. The unexpected contact startled her and she jumped in sudden alarm, a strangled squeak escaping from her throat but quickly brought in check. A dozen feet away Buddy continued his slumber undisturbed.

She bent close so she could whisper into his ear softly enough that there would be no likelihood of waking her son. "You're a nice man, Mr. Long."

"Miz Fulton, if you've woke me up just so you could tell me that . . ."

"Please, Mr. Long."

"Sorry." He decided maybe it wasn't teasing she was needing here in the middle of the night.

"It has been . . . I can't tell you how terribly, terribly long it has been since anyone has been . . . nice to me. I mean, genuinely nice, really and truly nice, just to *be* nice. I mean, not because they're wanting anything out of it but just to be really, really *nice*. And to Eric too. That means so much to me, Mr. Long, I just can't tell you . . ."

"There's nothing you got to tell, Miz Fulton, nor nothing you got to do."

"You see," she whispered. "That's just exactly what I mean. And I just . . . would you mind doing me a favor, Mr. Long?"

"Anything I reasonably can, ma'am."

"Would you . . . hold me? Please? Not screw me, see. Lots of men do that. But just . . . hold me? Like a man does with a woman and not like a sport does with a whore?"

Longarm's answer was easy enough. He reached up and put his arms around this plain, sad little woman, drawing her down onto his chest and pulling her to him.

Her weight atop him was little more than a thick quilt would have been, and her breath was warm and ticklish against the side of his neck. He held her so as to comfort rather than arouse her. At first her slim body was atremble. Slowly her quaking lessened, and finally disappeared. Her breathing slowed, and after a bit she wriggled a little, seeking a more comfortable position. Longarm slowly, gently stroked the back of her head.

Her hair had been loosened and allowed to fall free. It felt cool and silky to the touch. And her body . . . he frowned, angry with himself. If there was anything Buddy Fulton's mama did not need right now, it was the feel of a hard-on poking her in the belly. That wasn't what she had come here to find, and . . .

He first felt, then softly heard a chuckle forming low in her throat and rocking her whole small body as she tried to contain it.

"What's so funny?" he whispered.

"You."

"Me! What the hell did I do?"

"Oh, it's just that you are such a . . . how can I put this that I won't offend you? Just that you are such a *man*."

"Somehow I got the notion you don't mean that like it sounds. An' anyway, it occurs to me that there ain't a whole hell of a lot I can do about it."

"Oh, you know what I mean."

"Do I?"

"Of course you do. There's something warm and soft pressed against you, so that blind snake of yours stands up and looks around trying to find the way in. That isn't what you had in mind, of course. I know that. All you wanted to do right now was to hold me and be nice to me. Because like I said, Mr. Long, you are a very nice man. A truly good and decent man, I think. But here I am, lying on top of you, and you don't have any control over your own reaction. Your prick is trying to stand at attention and salute, and you're trying to keep it from getting that way. It's really kind of funny. And cute. And . . . anyway, that's what I mean about you being a man. You can't help yourself. And I can't help it if I think it's kind of funny and kind of cute."

"I ain't entirely sure, Miz Fulton, but I think I been a little bit complimented outa one side of your mouth an' just the least little bit insulted outa the other." He laughed, the rise and fall of his belly carrying her with it like a small boat on a restive sea.

"A little of both perhaps," she conceded.

And then, with a murmur and a smile, she kissed the side of his neck.

"Miz Fulton, really, you don't gotta . . ."

"Mr. Long. Please. I know that I don't have to. It's just that . . . for the first time in ever so long . . . I really would like to. Not for money. I understand what you did earlier, and it has nothing to do with this. It is just that this is a gift I am able to give to you. If you are willing to accept it."

"Yes," he said solemnly, sensing that this gift she was offering meant much more than she might be willing to let on. "I would like that very much, Miz Fulton."

"Could I say one thing then?"

"Anything."

"Under these, um, circumstances, Mr. Long, don't you think you should stop being so formal and just call me Angela now?"

He laughed. "If you'll stop callin' me mister."

"All right. But I have to tell you. . ."

"Yes?"

"I've forgotten your first name."

He laughed harder this time and gave her a quick, fierce hug. Damned if Mrs. Fulton—Angela, that is—wasn't turning out to be a very nice little woman.

And a direct one too. Practically before the whispering had a chance to die away her hand was investigating his drawers, pushing and tugging and sliding him free of the restraints of the cloth.

Still on top and straddling him with her warm, slim body, Angela pulled the hem of her nightgown high.

Longarm was plenty ready by then. She lifted herself over him and, pausing for a moment, swiftly speared herself on the erect pole of his manhood.

Angela gasped lightly as she felt the immense length of him fill her.

"Are you . . . ?"

"Yes, shhh, don't wake Eric."

Waking the boy wasn't exactly what he had on his mind at the moment. Damn but Angela did feel warm and wet around him. "Jeez," he groaned.

"Shhh," she warned again.

"Yeah, right, whatever."

Angela adjusted her position, drawing her legs up so that she was almost squatting over him. She leaned forward a little with her fingertips spread wide and both hands braced on the hard flat of his chest. He wasn't sure, but thought she was humming to herself very, very softly as his cock burrowed balls-deep inside her.

Then, in time to some inner rhythm that only she could hear, Angela Fulton began to rise and fall with all the slow, inexorable power and insistence of the tide.

When once Longarm tried to move, tried to meet her motion with a thrust of his own, she clucked her tongue and shook her head to stop him.

"Let me," she whispered. "Let this be my gift to you."

And so he subsided and lay quiescent and accepting as Angela lifted and fell, lifted and fell . . . and gently, inevitably pulled the hot, liquid life force from him.

As the sensations she was giving him built one on top of another, accumulating like snow adhering to a ball rolled from the top of a steep hill, Longarm closed his eyes and arched his back, lifting both of them off the floor while Angela's movements became faster, faster, harder and deeper.

She was panting now and bucking up and down with frantic urgency.

He could feel the clutch and the pull of her thighs clamped hard against his sides and the dripping heat of her body engulfing him.

Angela began to whimper and groan, all thoughts of her son nearby forgotten for the moment, and Longarm felt a wave of powerful convulsions sweep through her. Her body rocked and quivered, and the lips of her pussy clamped tight around him as a powerful climax surged through her.

The feel of her pleasure clutching so hard and hot around him was enough and more than enough to tip him over the edge so that he too went rigid as a drawn bowstring. He felt the flooding eruption of pleasure gather deep in his cods and race the length of his cock to spew out in one pulsing gush after another, the seed of his body spilling deep inside hers, gluing the two into one if only for that brief instant in time.

Longarm shuddered, only dimly aware of Angela's own tremors of pleasure.

And then, gentle once again, he drew her down onto his sweaty chest. He could feel the flutter of her racing heartbeat soft against his body and the flow of her breath warm on his throat.

He took a slow, deep breath and lightly stroked the back of her head. "Wow," he whispered.

"Mmm. Yeah. Really wow," she mumbled, the contentment like honey in her voice.

He continued to pet and stroke her, and after a bit could feel her body go lax and utterly limp on his. Her breathing slowed, and soon he knew she was asleep.

Longarm closed his eyes. He would have to wake her before morning to make sure Buddy didn't get up and catch the two of them together like this.

But there was time enough to think about that later.

For right now this was . . . nice. It was even quite special. Longarm certainly was in no hurry to let go of this great and wondrous gift Angela Fulton had bestowed upon him.

He smiled into the night and continued to stroke Angela's hair even though he knew perfectly well she no longer consciously felt it. He smiled. And after a time he slept.

Chapter 17

"You cocksucker!"

"It's nice to see you too, Harry." Longarm hung his Stetson on a peg and helped himself to a seat on one of the two chairs that crowded the Cargyle police chief's tiny office. He was able to manage both without taking his eyes off Bolt. Just in case. Not that he expected anything untoward to happen before breakfast. But with a man like Harry . . .

Harry Bolt—former deputy United States marshal, former undersheriff for Animas County, Colorado, former night marshal at Trinidad, former . . . there were lots of jobs Longarm knew Bolt had held—was a beefy man with the red-veined complexion of a heavy drinker and the bulging belly of a dedicated eater. A good many men had thought Harry Bolt's appearance was that of a man who'd gone slow and soft. Those men had been wrong. And more often than not they'd paid for their error with spilled blood, broken bones, or worse.

Bolt had thinning gray hair, a gold tooth in the middle of his jaw, and a pipsqueak Smith Wesson rimfire .32 revolver that he wore on his belly to the right of his belt buckle. The gun looked too small and inoffensive to be threatening. Much of the nickel plating on it had worn off to be replaced with rust, and the front sight was missing. Practically no one took the gun seriously. Except Longarm. He had seen what Harry Bolt and that idiotic, two-bit popgun of his could accomplish. Not fast, mind. No one can be fast with a rimfire Smith & Wesson. But Harry Bolt was hell for accurate, and in a real-life gunfight deliberate accuracy beats a fast noise every time.

Longarm didn't underestimate Harry Bolt.

Didn't like the son of a bitch either.

Which, of course, was neither here nor there so far as this assignment was concerned.

Before Longarm could tell Bolt what that assignment was, the Cargyle police chief spat in the general direction of a filthy cuspidor and growled, "You wouldn't've been messing around at Cletus Terry's hog ranch last night, would you?"

"I don't recall ever meeting anybody by that name." Longarm glanced idly around the tiny building that served as jail and police station alike here. There was no sign of the prisoner who'd been in the one cell the previous evening. At the moment Longarm and Bolt were alone.

"Clete runs one of the joints down by the gate," Bolt said. "Big fella, Clete is. Said some smartass son of a bitch sucker-punched him last night and then backed it up with a gun. When he said smartass son of a bitch, Long, it shoulda been description enough for me to know it was you."

Longarm snorted. "This Terry fella. He think he's a big man with a knife? Hell on hot wheels when it comes to scaring little-bitty women?"

"See? I knew it was you. Soon as I seen you walk through that door I knew it was you."

"The man's an idiot, Bolt. Almost as stupid as you are. He's an idiot an' a liar too."

"The biggest difference between him and me, Long, is that you wouldn't be able to take me like you took Clete. You see, he don't know you like I do. Me you couldn't take by surprise like you done him."

90

"Look, Harry, I didn't come here to lock horns with you."
There was no point in trying to explain what really happened
last night, Longarm knew. Harry wouldn't believe him anyway. Hell, he wouldn't want to believe him. Better to just let
that go. "I came here to save your worthless ass. Not my idea,
mind, so don't get all upset thinking you might have to thank
me. I'm here on official business."

"So lay it out and get the hell outa here before I run you in
for disturbing the peace."

Longarm gave Bolt a smartass grin, the most deliberately
smartass expression he could manage since it seemed to be
smartass that Bolt was expecting here, and said, "On a warrant
sworn out by your pal Terry? Go ahead, Bolt. Feel free."

"What, you ain't gonna bluster about what you'll do to me
if I take you in?"

"It never makes sense to get into a kicking contest with a
mule, Bolt. I learned that real young. No, you go ahead an'
do whatever you think is best. Then I'll do the same."

Bolt shifted a mite on his chair, then leaned forward with
a frown. Whatever he might have been thinking, he thought
better of it now. "Just get your business tended to, Long. And
get the hell outa my town."

Longarm took out a cheroot that he nipped and trimmed and
fired up with slow deliberation. And without offering one to
Harry.

Then, when he was quite good and ready, he explained about
Steven Reese and the murders of the Last Man Club members.

"I suppose you remember the kid, Bolt. Of course he woulda
been just a little knocker then."

Harry Bolt spat toward his cuspidor again—he wasn't much
for accuracy in that regard, though he would have to receive
high marks for volume and enthusiasm—and gave a wave of
dismissal as if none of this particularly concerned him.

"I don't recollect any kid. But shit, you know me. I don't
even pay attention to my own kids. If I got any, ha-ha. The

little bastards aren't any account. Not the boys, ha-ha. As for the girls, well, there ain't nothing wrong with young snatch, right, ha-ha? Big enough to bleed is big enough to butcher. Ain't that right?"

Longarm chose to ignore that crude comment. After all, what else could be expected of someone like Bolt? "You do recall the daddy, don't you? This Ellis Reese? They tell me him an' his boy lived at the same post as you before the army brought charges against Reese. And the Last Man Club, Harry. You do remember that, don't you?"

"Yeah, sure. But that's been a long time back. You know? All bullshit, that's what it is. This Reese kid, if he really is going around trying to make his daddy rich or something, he won't mess with me. I'd drill a hole square between his goddamn eyes if he was to come around here."

"You seem sure of yourself, Harry."

"That's because I am, Long. I ain't scared and you know it. Got no reason to be. If this Reese bastard's kid comes around—or you, Long—or any-damn-body else, I'll put their pimply asses in the cold, hard ground. And you know I can do it."

Longarm frowned. But didn't bother to challenge the imbecile.

There would be no point in it.

He did, however, feel duty bound to say, "Don't forget, Harry. The kid will remember you from back when you were already grown. You'll have gotten older, but won't have changed all that much since he was a boy. He on the other hand will've done his growing up since then. There's a good chance that he'll remember you but you won't have no way to spot him. He could be just another young face in the crowd. But you, you'll stand out to him. He'll know you as soon as he sees you."

Harry Bolt clouded up and looked like he was going to bust clean apart from the blood that rushed into his already drink-flushed and ruddy face. "Get outa here. I won't warn you again."

Longarm stood and retrieved his Stetson from the peg where he'd hung it. "I'm asking you official now, Harry, which you know I got to do. Do you as chief of the Cargyle, Colorado, police request assistance from the United States marshal's office in protecting you, or anyone else, from the murder suspect known as Steven Reese?"

"The only thing I want from you, Long, is to see your ass headed outa my town. Right the hell now."

"Yeah, sure. Nice to see you again too, Harry." Longarm set the Stetson comfortably in place, dropped the butt of his cigar onto Bolt's jail floor, and carefully ground it out beneath the heel of his boot.

Harry Bolt glowered but didn't say anything.

Without another word Longarm turned and got the hell out of there before he did something that Billy Vail would be ashamed of him for.

Chapter 18

That, Longarm figured, just about covered the subject. After all, it wasn't his responsibility to find or arrest or stop or otherwise deal with Steven Reese. Billy and his pompous lawyer friend had sent Longarm down here to warn Harry Bolt. Well, he'd done that. And the plain truth of the matter was that he wasn't very much inclined to offer to do any more. Bolt was well and truly warned and that was the end of it. Longarm could collect his things from Angela Fulton's place—sweet, sweet little woman, Angela; he would have enjoyed an excuse to stay there another night or two—and head back to Denver.

He figured he would get Buddy to drive him out to the main line again. Once there, he could signal for a passenger pickup on the next northbound. Considering how early it still was, the sun barely high enough to reach into the canyon here, although still low enough to sneak in underneath the brim of his hat and sting his eyes, he should be able to make it all the way home in one day. With any kind of luck at all he should be sleeping in his own bed tonight.

He sauntered along the tracks of the railroad spur, crossed the creek on a flimsy foot bridge—the wagon road and even the rails were laid over a bed of solid stone that had a few inches of sluggish water covering it—and ambled on past the invisible "gate" that separated the coal company's land from the squatters' community.

Longarm's belly growled a mite, reminding him that he hadn't gotten around to eating yet this morning. He wondered if he should ask Angela to cook something for him or if he would be better off to go on past in search of a cafe. After last night it would be awkward to try and pay Angela for a meal now. And anything she would be able to provide without him going out and doing some shopping for her would likely be on the order of oatmeal or fried mush, something cheap and filling. If he went on by and found a cafe, he could wrap himself around something more substantial than that. And the simple truth was that his hankerings this morning ran more toward pork chops and eggs than to rolled oats and cold biscuits.

He walked on past the Fulton shack without so much as slowing down, and had no trouble at all finding a cafe capable of satisfying his desires.

Afterward he fired up a cheroot and walked next door to stop in at the local barber's. He hadn't shaved yet this morning, and was thinking ahead to later in the day when there just might be some interesting fillies aboard the train into Denver. A fella never knows what he might run into when he travels. He fingered his chin and asked, "You got time for one more?"

"If you got the dime, mister, I got the time. Come right in and set over there. There's only two gentlemen ahead of you."

Longarm took the offered seat and browsed through a Pueblo paper that he hadn't read before. There were several Denver papers available too, but every one of them was old enough that he'd already read them before he ever left on this trip south.

The barber was as good as his word, and in less than twenty minutes Longarm's face was layered in hot towels while the barber went to work stropping his razor and whipping up a renewed froth in his soap mug.

There is, Longarm reflected, damn little that can put a man so much at ease as a good, old-fashioned barbershop shave. It's one of the few opportunities a man has in this life to let himself be pampered and fussed over and yet not be mistaken for some sort of priss-ass dandy.

He closed his eyes and let the homey sounds of the shop surround him.

He was about half asleep when harsh noise intruded on his reverie.

"Mr. Sam, come quick, will ya, please, will ya, my ma's been hurt awful bad and I don't know what to do for her, please, Mr. Sam, you got to come help her, she's bleeding something terrible and I can't get it to stop and——"

Longarm opened his eyes and sat upright in the barber chair.

That was Buddy Fulton talking, he saw. And that meant. . . *shit!*

The barber had already set the soap mug aside and was headed out the door with a small black case tucked under one arm.

Longarm yanked the apron off his lap and stood, damp towels spilling unnoticed onto the floor from the loose wrap around his jowls.

Buddy was leading the way at a run and the barber scurried to keep up.

Longarm's long legs brought him quickly to the barber's side.

"Mister, you don't have to——"

"I know the woman, friend. In fact I'm boarding at her house, with her and Buddy."

"Oh. All right then."

"Come on, dammit," Longarm urged. "The boy said she's bleeding." And he broke into a run.

Chapter 19

Angela Fulton looked like she'd stepped in front of a runaway beer wagon.

Her nose was broken and her left eye was puffed completely shut. Her right eye had been reduced to little more than a blue and purple slit in the side of her face. Or what remained of her face. At the moment it was hardly recognizable as one.

Most of the teeth on the left side of her mouth were so loose Longarm would have considered them gone, but the barber— the closest thing Cargyle had to a doctor, and fortunately a real barber with proper barber/surgeon schooling—claimed they would all tighten up and be saved if she wasn't beaten on anymore for the next month or so.

"Oh, she won't be beaten up no more, friend. I can promise you that," Longarm said with heat in his voice.

The barber grunted, but didn't otherwise comment on the rashness of Longarm's statement. He just went on with his work, which at the moment was mostly concerned with stanching the flow of blood from Angela's nose and left ear.

The heavy bleeding from the nose he stopped by taking a scrap of cloth little bigger than a good-sized postage stamp and rolling it into a tiny, sausage-shaped bundle. He pulled on Angela's upper lip the way you will lift a mare's lip to check her teeth, and tucked the cloth wadding tight against her gum just as high as he could force it.

"Keep that there, Mrs. Fulton. It will feel strange, but the veins going into your nose pass over the bone at that spot. If you can keep the pressure on right there for just five or ten minutes, the blood on the surface will clot and the bleeding will stop."

Longarm wasn't at all sure Angela was conscious enough for the barber's instructions to register. But she didn't spit out the cloth wadding, so maybe she was aware of her surroundings after all.

The man examined her ear, and cleaned it out as best he could with some bits of cotton speared on the end of a smooth stick. He didn't look particularly happy when he was done there even though the bleeding had stopped, pretty much on its own.

"Too soon to say if she'll lose the hearing in that ear or not. Could go either way."

Longarm scowled but didn't say anything.

"Buddy, was your mama hit in the stomach or the chest area?"

"I dunno, Mr. Sam. I wasn't here. I'd gone out to the Parker farm to get the day's milk and bring it in, me and Peppy." Peppy, or had he said Pepe? Not that it mattered. After a moment Longarm remembered that was Buddy's pony. "I took it to the store the same as usual and came back here just a coupla minutes ago. I found her just like you see now, Mr. Sam. Is she gonna be all right, Mr. Sam?"

"She's going to be just fine, Buddy. But I need for you and the gentleman here to step outside now. I have to look your mama over to see if she's hurt anyplace we can't see. I'm thinking she probably has some busted ribs, so I'll have to wrap her tight to take away some of the hurting. But I won't know that for sure until I examine her. Now you scoot outside, Buddy. And you too, Mister . . . ?"

It was a poor time for introductions, but Longarm gave his name and took Buddy outside. They stood close to the door. Longarm had a cigar to fiddle with to occupy his hands if not his thoughts. Poor little Buddy didn't have that much of a distraction. Twice they heard Angela cry out in pain, quickly followed by Sam the Barber's soothing comments to her.

"Buddy?"

"Yes, sir?"

"You got any idea who might've done this to your mama or why?"

"No, sir. I can't think of nobody that don't like my ma. She gets along with most everybody."

Except at least one person, Longarm amended silently.

"Did you see anyone on the street when you and, uh, Peppy were coming back home? Anybody going toward town from down this way?"

"Just Mr. Terry. But he wouldn't . . . Mr. Long, can I tell you a secret? It's something . . . promise me if I tell that you won't tell nobody else. Not never."

"I won't tell anyone if there's any way I can keep from it, son. I can make you that promise."

"I just . . . you remember what that damn Rick said yesterday?"

It took Longarm a few seconds to recall who Rick was. And what he'd said. "Oh, yes. Now I remember."

"Well, what he said . . . Ma does work for Mr. Terry over at the saloon. I don't know what she does there, but she don't want me to know about it. I don't think it's real bad like that damn Rick says. But it's something she don't talk about. Not to me. Anyway, she like . . . kinda works for Mr. Terry. So I wouldn't think he'd hurt her. Do you?" The boy gave Longarm a deeply troubled look.

"I can't see why he would want to hurt your mother whether or not she works for him sometimes," Longarm said smoothly. It came out slick as snot on ice. But it was a lie through and

99

through. Longarm could think of exactly why Mr. Cletus Terry would beat up on Angela Fulton this morning.

After all, that poor, sweet woman had seen Mister Musclehead's nose rubbed in the dirt last night. And by a man who hadn't even raised a sweat in doing it.

She'd seen him humiliated and for some bullies—and Lord knows Cletus Terry seemed to qualify for that designation—that was enough of an excuse and more than enough.

Longarm's eyes narrowed as he drew smoke deep into his lungs, held it, and slowly let it trickle out again.

Cletus Terry. Entrepreneur and respected businessman hereabouts. Chummy with Harry Bolt. Which meant there was no way, never a chance, that anything—*any*thing—Clete Terry might choose to do to, with, or about Angela Fulton would ever get the man in trouble with what passed for the law in Cargyle.

And wasn't that a shame.

Longarm finished his cheroot and tossed it onto the ground.

"Mister? You don't think she'll die, do you?"

Longarm gave Buddy a startled look. Good Lord, the kid all this time had been thinking that?

"No, son. Your mama isn't going to die." His eyes narrowed. "She isn't going to be hurt anymore either."

"Mister," the barber called out. "Could you come here for a minute? I can't get this tape wound tight enough by myself."

"Wait here, Buddy. We'll talk some more when I come out again. And don't you worry none. Your mama is gonna be all right now. I promise."

Chapter 20

Longarm didn't recognize the day man behind the bar at Cletus Terry's saloon. Didn't have any quarrel with him either. The man, at least as far as Longarm knew, had had nothing to do with the beating of Angela Fulton.

"Yes, what will it be this morning?"

Longarm took his time about answering, first taking a slow look around the place. At this hour he was the only customer there.

It's funny, he reflected, how different a saloon looks at night when it's busy as opposed to the morning hours when harsh daylight points out all the peeling paint and unsightly scuff marks.

There is even a different smell to a saloon at such times. At night the smell is a lively, active thing—tobacco smoke, sweat, beer, and good times—while in the day a saloon smells empty and stale. By morning's light all the scent has leeched out of the spilled whiskey and beer, leaving behind only a weary stink like a dim memory of past pleasures. Helluva difference, Longarm thought as he leaned one elbow on the bar, standing sideways so that he could keep an eye on the big empty room. Just in case.

"Was there something . . . ?" The bartender sounded a mite uncertain.

Longarm brought his thoughts back to the moment and gave the man a nod and a reassuring smile. "Sorry, friend. I was wool-gatherin'."

The bartender's smile looked to be just the least little bit relieved. After all, he didn't know Longarm—or this tall stranger's intentions—any more than Longarm knew him.

"I'd like a beer," Longarm said. "And d'you have any good cigars? I favor cheroots if you have them."

"The beer I can do, but the only cigars I have are these rum crooks." He reached beneath the counter and brought a wooden box into view. It was a cigar box, all right, but the dark, rum-soaked things that were tumbled into the box hadn't been packed there by any factory. Or whatever the hell you call a place where cigars are rolled. The crooks were the sort that came shipped in kegs. Cheap. "Three for a nickel," the bartender confirmed.

"I'll have the beer then and a nickel's worth of those"— Longarm grinned—"good cigars."

The bartender chuckled and drew the beer. He let Longarm select his own handful of sticky, tacky crooks. The grade of tobacco used in such smokes was so bad, so bitter, that the cigars had to be soaked in a syrup of rum and molasses in an attempt to sweeten the flavor and mask the bite of the truly awful tobacco leaf.

Longarm laid a coin on the bar, pocketed his change, and carried mug and stogies alike to a table at the side of the big room.

He paused for a moment to look things over, then judiciously moved the table a few feet deeper into the front corner of the building. He took one of the chairs and turned it so the back was close to the side wall, pulled the chair a few inches forward to give himself room to comfortably rock backward, then settled

102

himself into place beside the table without once touching either beer or cigar.

The bartender gave him a quizzical look. And then as quickly looked away as if trying to convince the gentleman that, no, he hadn't been staring. He sure hadn't been.

Longarm didn't give a shit if the man stared at him or not. Before this day was out he figured there would be stares aplenty.

"What are you doing here, mister? Just what the hell do you think you are *doing* here?"

Longarm took his time responding, first very slowly and thoroughly looking over the clientele that was beginning to drift in for a quick drink over the noon hour, then as slowly—and as unblinking as a lizard in the desert heat—bringing his eyes to bear on the saloon keeper. Longarm's eyes bored into the man like the blank, gaping tubes of a double-barrel shotgun taking careful aim. "I'm having a beer, of course. And a smoke." His voice was as slow and deliberate as his stare.

"Jesus God, mister, you been here two, three hours now and you haven't touched that beer yet. Or any of them cigars. What is it with you?"

"Work on it, Terry. It'll come to you."

"But—"

"Even to a man as stupid as you if you work on it."

There were several patrons close enough to overhear—for sure Longarm wasn't making any attempt to keep his voice down—and those who did began to pay attention to the conversation that was taking place nearby. They nudged the elbows of their neighbors, and so on down the line until nearly the entire lunch crowd was doing its silent best to eavesdrop on this unexpected confrontation.

"Listen, you sonuvabitch, you get out of here. Right now. You hear me? Out."

Longarm's expression never changed. Nor did the unblinking focus of his stare.

Cletus Terry licked his lips and glanced nervously about. He was beginning to sense that this thing—whatever the hell it was—was going beyond his ability to understand, much less to control. And he seemed to sense as well that he was no longer alone with this man, that all the men in the place were listening and watching too.

"Look, uh, if it's about last night, mister, I, uh, I apologize. All right? I was out of line. I admit that, okay? But there wasn't no harm done. Right?"

Longarm didn't answer. And didn't look away. He continued to sit there, hands folded across his belly and chair tipped lazily against the wall, and look bold and cold into Clete Terry's nervously skittish eyes.

Anyone looking on was welcome to notice, if he wished, that the position of Longarm's chair prevented anyone from coming up behind him. And that the casual placement of his arms kept his gun hand within two or three inches of the butt of the .44 Colt revolver that lay in a cross-draw rig on his belly.

"So what the hell do you want here anyway?" Clete Terry demanded, loudly this time as his anger—and possibly some niggling intimation of fear as well—began to germinate and grow.

Longarm said nothing. He only sat. And silently, coldly stared.

"All right, dammit. I don't care. You're done. You hear me? You're done. Get out. Get out right now." Terry grabbed up the full but by now warm and flat beer, slopping much of it onto the table. With his other hand he grabbed up the rum crooks, looked at them as if wondering how the hell they'd gotten into his grip, and slammed them down onto the table again hard enough to break them and scatter lumpy bits of blackened tobacco into the previously spilled beer. "Get out, I tell you. Get out."

Longarm said nothing. He simply watched.

Over at the bar the patrons began to speak among themselves. But in whispers now and with frequent glances in Longarm's direction.

Going behind the bar Clete Terry, his face red and puffy with fury, hissed instructions to his daytime bartender, then stormed away into the back-room depths of the building.

Longarm sat calmly where he was, chair pushed back and hands folded on his stomach. He didn't so much as look in the direction of the spilled beer and shattered cigars on the table.

He simply . . . sat.

And watched.

And waited.

Chapter 21

Longarm watched the pair of plug-uglies slink toward him like a pair of rattlesnakes sidling up to a packrat. The difference, of course, was that he wasn't a packrat. And these boys didn't have quite the fangs that they thought they did.

"You boys get it worked out what Terry's to pay you if you get rid o' me?" he said in greeting.

"We don't know what you're talking about, mister."

"I'll tell you a truth, friend. The man that don't know what he's talking about here is your friend Clete Terry. An' don't bother denyin' what we all know. I seen you over there whispering to him a minute ago. So did everybody else in the bar. The only real question now is whether his offer is good enough to be worth dyin' over."

The thick-shouldered coal miner on the right gave his pal a worried glance.

"What's the matter?" Longarm asked. "Terry never mentioned the possibility o' dyin'? He should've."

"We just . . ."

"You just was told to throw some muscle around an' move me out o' here, right?"

The man on the left shrugged. He was a little smaller

than his chum and a few pounds lighter, but didn't look any brighter. Or cleaner, for that matter. Both of them were in serious need of a bath and a shave before they would fit in among polite company.

"Let me show you a couple things before you decide how bad you want the money," Longarm suggested.

Without waiting for an answer he first took hold of the butt of his Colt. He didn't draw the gun. But then he didn't figure he would have to.

"That's one," he said. "An' the other." He reached inside his coat and pulled out the wallet he sometimes carried there, flipping it open to display the badge identifying him as a United States deputy marshal. He gave the boys a glimpse but not reading privileges, closing the wallet and returning it to his pocket quickly. "What I'm doin' here, fellas, is official business. If you wanta press your luck far enough to interfere with that business, feel free. You're all grown up now, an' you can do whatever you think best. But I oughta tell you. I ain't in no mood to be fooled with. The very least you'd get out of it would be jail an' a trip to Denver for prosecution in federal court. Prob'ly a sentence of one to three years in a federal pen. With time off for good behavior you won't likely have to serve more'n nine, ten months actual behind-bars time. That's if things go good for you. At the worst, like if I feel things are gettin' outa hand, I shoot an' call it self-defense. But like I said, you boys feel free to do whatever you're of a mind to. I'll be right here waitin' if you want to go talk it over between you."

"Mister, uh, there ain't no need for that," the one on the left said.

"Clete, he's only offering drinks," the other one put in. "I never yet had that much of a thirst on me."

"I appreciate your point of view," Longarm said.

"No hard feelings, mister?"

"None on my end," Longarm assured them.

The would-be bullyboys went back across the room, whispered briefly between themselves, and concluded they might be more comfortable buying their after-shift drinks somewhere else.

Longarm's gut was rumbling in protest of the shoddy treatment he was imposing on it. Hell, here it was past the evening dinner hour and he hadn't yet had lunch. He was hungry, and if he didn't go take a leak pretty soon his bladder was going to bust wide open.

Still, his presence was having the desired effect. Clete Terry was about to go out of his goddamn mind at the brooding, silently ominous presence that was disrupting business.

Oh, there were plenty of people in the saloon this evening, that was for sure. The place was crowded. But nobody was saying much and nobody was drinking much. The gaming tables stood empty and quiet, and the whores were staying out of sight. The entertainment of the evening was Custis Long. And the reaction Clete Terry was having to him.

It was a good thing Longarm didn't mind being stared at.

"Thank God," Terry blurted aloud, along toward half past seven. The saloon keeper's expression broke into smiling relief, and he rushed across the crowded room to greet his savior at the door.

Longarm would have been able to guess without looking that Harry Bolt was on hand. The only question was what had kept Harry away this long.

Still, although he didn't show it, Longarm was almost as glad to have Bolt finally arrive as Terry obviously was.

Although in truth Longarm's reason was somewhat different from Terry's.

Clete Terry wanted his asshole buddy Harry to take care of the problem for him.

What Longarm wanted was for Terry to find out that he didn't have the threat of Harry Bolt's badge to prop him up.

This one Terry would have to work out by himself. He just didn't know that yet.

Terry looked quickly around, but he and Bolt were the objects of the attention of virtually every man in the place. They wouldn't be able to whisper a damn thing without at least one eavesdropper hearing what it was. And spreading it to everyone else.

The saloon keeper took Harry Bolt by the sleeve and tugged him off into the back room where they could talk in private.

Bolt, Longarm was pleased to notice, saw who it was who was causing the problem before his pal Terry got him out of sight. Clete Terry might not like it—and for that matter neither would Harry Bolt—but Harry would know that there wouldn't be any getting around it. If Longarm wanted to claim he was sitting there under the authority of official business, there was nothing Bolt's local jurisdiction could do about it.

Not really. Not when Harry's bosses at Great Western Coal and Coke depended on federal mining leases to make their profits. If there was anybody the mining companies did not want to piss off it was the federal government.

And there wasn't any employee, not Harry Bolt or anybody else, valuable enough to make the big mining companies forget their own self-interest.

If push ever turned to shove, it would be Bolt who would be getting pushed. And Harry would understand that right good and well.

Longarm didn't like the son of a bitch one iota. But he knew that, unlike Cletus Terry, Harry was smart enough to test the direction of the wind before he started pissing into it.

Longarm sat right where he was.

And wished to hell his bladder wouldn't hurt so much. Lordy, but he did have to take a leak. And his mouth felt cotton dry from being so thirsty, yet if he got himself something to drink now, that would only add to the other discomforts.

He continued to sit there, silent and without words, while

109

the saloon filled with a soft, buzzing drone of low voices.

The night bartender almost jumped out of his skin when the back room door opened and Cargyle Police Chief Harry Bolt came out, his always ruddy complexion almost purple with anger now. Harry glowered at the men who were waiting for a chance to see a flurry of raw, sudden violence. Then stalked out of the place without a word to anyone.

Behind him Clete Terry came into view and stepped up onto an overturned box to loudly address Longarm and every other man in the room.

Chapter 22

"We're closed, boys. Closed for the night. I'm sorry, but that man over there is looking for trouble. He wants to gun somebody down and pretend it's legal. And he won't even say why. Well, we aren't going to put up with it. Chief Bolt tells me the sensible thing to do here is to shut down and just not give him no excuses to fly off the handle, so that's what we are going to do. We're closed for the night now, boys. Sorry. But I want you all to go home now. Go on. Everybody out." Terry motioned to the bartender, who immediately began extinguishing the lamps he'd lighted only minutes earlier.

There was a murmuring among the men. Then the crowd began to disperse as they realized there would be no violence tonight. And no other form of fun either. Bar and tables alike were, and would remain, closed.

Once the flow toward the door began, the place quickly emptied, leaving Longarm alone with just the bartender for company. Clete Terry had already disappeared into the back of his saloon again.

Longarm sat a moment longer, quietly smiling to himself while he reached for the cheroot he'd been craving for at least the past five hours.

Then he stood, his knees creaking after the long hours of immobility, and stretched. He let out a resounding fart, yawned, and scratched himself.

First stop, he figured, would be into the nearest outhouse to relieve himself. Then something, anything, wet to pour down his gullet. Hell, even water would do. He was that desperate. From there . . . from there he'd work it out.

"Good night," he called pleasantly to the bartender as he left the gapingly empty saloon at what should have been its busiest hour.

Angela Fulton looked like shit. To be more accurate about it, she looked like a piece of raw meat. Her face was swollen and discolored to the point that it didn't overmuch look like a human face anymore.

On the other hand, she was alive, she was conscious, and she was needing her strength.

Longarm was pleased to see a spark of interest in her eyes— at least those were unchanged, although the red and purple surroundings made it a trifle difficult to judge that fact—when he took the lid off the pot he was carrying and the rich, steamy aroma filled the small room.

Buddy was plenty interested too, of course, but hell, Longarm had known that would be so. Young boys always think they're on the fringes of total starvation.

"I brought some chicken broth with whipped egg yolks swirled in. That's almighty good for whatever ails a body. An' the lady at the cafe said I should bring you some o' this clabbered milk. It smells like . . . well, I ain't gonna say out loud what it smells like. But she claims you like it an' that it's every bit as good for you as the soup will be."

Angela nodded weakly.

With Buddy's help Longarm got her propped more or less upright on a mound of pillows. "Son, whyn't you fetch me a spoon. An' a towel or cloth of some kind too. Your mama

112

looks to me like a messy eater. Reckon we gotta be prepared to mop up whatever spills. An' before you get all down in the mouth 'bout your prospects for supper, soon as your mama is all set for me to feed her, you can dig inta that hamper over on the table there. I brung some fried chicken and other chewable fixings for you an' me. All right?"

"All *right*!" Buddy yipped as he jumped to help with the tasks Longarm had set him.

"How you doin'?" Longarm asked softly while the boy's attention was elsewhere.

Angela managed a small shrug and a hint of a nod. She wasn't feeling worth crap, of course, but she was making it. Longarm supposed that under the circumstances that was really pretty good.

Buddy handed him the spoon and towel he'd asked for.

"You go ahead an' eat while it's still hot," Longarm said. He grinned and added, "But mind you save me more'n your chewed-over bones, hear?"

Not that there was much worry about that. He'd brought enough chicken, biscuits, and other eatables to feed four grown men. That, he figured, should be just about right for one man and a boy.

"Yessir," Buddy quickly agreed, and scampered off to the table.

Longarm chuckled a mite at the kid's enthusiasm, then set himself to the slow, patient task of feeding Angela a teaspoon or so of broth at a time.

Chapter 23

Longarm wasn't so rash the second day as he'd been the first. This time he thought to do a little planning ahead. For one thing he waited until lunchtime before he showed up at the saloon. The early morning hours weren't busy ones anyway, and they'd been annoying to sit through for nothing. Making his appearance during the lunch hour, though, should put a serious crimp in Clete Terry's business.

He also made sure he was physically prepared, or as close to it as he could get, to spend however long it took sitting there like a vulture waiting to swoop down and gobble something up. For openers he made sure he was well watered and also well drained before he ever walked through the door, and that his belly was full. He smoked a last, good cheroot and then sauntered into Terry's saloon like he didn't have a care in the world.

"Oh, shit," the daytime bartender said by way of a welcome.

"And a fine good morning to you too, old son." Longarm leaned on the bar and looked around. There were two patrons bellied up to the free lunch spread at the far end of the bar. The nearer of them took one look at Longarm and left. The other man looked instead at the free lunch, plucked a slice of ham off the platter and dragged it through a bowl of mustard, and then he too turned and left the place at a slow lope.

"Not real busy so far today, are you?" Longarm said.

The bartender scowled at him but didn't offer any comments or suggestions. No doubt he'd received his instructions.

"I'd like a beer, please," Longarm said. "And three rum crooks."

The bartender delivered the merchandise and accepted payment. Longarm winked at him and carried his purchases to the table in the corner, where they would remain untouched for as long as he cared to sit there.

"The word is that you're yella, mister. They say you're all bluff and no huff."

"Is that so?" Longarm observed mildly. He smiled at the man while looking him over.

The belligerent butt-in was of average height or a little less, and couldn't have weighed more than 135 pounds at the very most. He had close-cropped black hair and the sort of deep, walnut tan that comes from spending day after day and week after week outdoors in hard sun.

This man was no coal miner, obviously. As for where he'd been . . . Longarm could figure that out without having to raise any sweat on his brain. The man was not long out of prison. Canon City most likely, considering where they were, although Yuma would also give a man that kind of extra deep tan. Most likely, though, he was a graduate of the Canon City rock pile, quarrying rock off the knife-edge mountain that lay behind the old territorial, now state penitentiary there, rock that would be used to construct still more cold, hostile, stone cell blocks.

Longarm knew the type, all right. Bitter and as hard and as cold as the stone he'd been breaking.

This man hadn't come looking for a fight or a payday. What he would be wanting was revenge. Revenge on anyone

115

in authority. And if that someone was a deputy marshal, why, so much the better.

Killing Longarm, ostensibly on behalf of Clete Terry, even though both he and Longarm would know Terry was only an excuse for violence here and no part of the real reason, would be something a man like this could savor and brag on for the rest of his days.

If, that is, he had any more days in which to brag.

He wore a gun that was long out of date—more evidence, as if any were needed, that he'd been out of circulation for a very long time—a .36 Colt Navy that had been converted to cartridge use. The loading ram had been removed and an ejector rod brazed in place beneath the slim barrel, and a loading gate had been attached behind the revamped cylinder. The gun would have been converted to a .38-caliber cartridge, either centerfire or rimfire depending on how long ago the conversion was done. The more powerful centerfire .38s hadn't been available when gunsmiths first started getting around patent restrictions by making the cartridge revolvers that the factories weren't allowed to produce.

Not that it mattered. Longarm was only postponing the inevitable by thinking over inconsequential details like that.

Better, he supposed, to go ahead and get this over with.

"They say you're a troublemaker," the ex-con accused.

"An' they'd be damn sure right about that," Longarm agreed.

"They say you eat shit for breakfast, dried and sliced with milk and sugar on it."

Longarm laughed. "Mister, I could claim you're the queen of England too. That wouldn't make it so. Or does that come close to home, huh? Were you inside that long? So tell me, which was you, the boy or the girl?"

The man clouded up and looked like he was fixing to rain all over himself. Which was just exactly what Longarm was wanting. Cold deliberation can be hard to deal with. But fury makes nearly any man easy prey, for it takes his judgment away and replaces it with unthinking reaction.

A deep flush turned the man's cheeks and neck dark, dark red, and his eyes bulged alarmingly.

His mouth opened and soundlessly gawped like a beached trout sucking air.

His right hand swept the Navy Colt out of the leather and on line with Longarm's belly.

At least, that was where the slender, lethal muzzle was heading and would have gone had it completed the ex-con's intentions.

Longarm wasn't much interested in allowing the fellow to shoot, though.

And for that matter wasn't really very keen on the notion of shooting him either.

Once the ex-con moved, so did Longarm.

Longarm was seated in his chair as usual, at the side of the table, the chair tipped back against the wall at a comfortable angle. The position was a natural one from which Longarm's boot snapped straight up at the same time the ex-con was dragging iron.

The toe of Longarm's boot slammed into the ex-con's knuckles just below the protection of the trigger guard on the old Colt. There was the muted, faintly brittle sound of bone breaking, and the ex-con cried out in sudden pain as his revolver went spinning end over end across the room. It landed in fresh sawdust and skittered to a halt.

By then Longarm was out of his chair with the ex-con's good hand pulled tight behind the man's back. Longarm pulled up on the arm, and the fellow had the choice of coming onto his tiptoes or standing firm and letting his elbow break. Sobbing, although probably more in rage and frustration than in pain, he gave in to the pressure.

"Y'know, old son, what I prob'ly ought to do here is give you a lesson in manners the old-fashioned way. You know how

117

I mean. Take my handcuffs and whip your face an' head with them until I'm too worn out to whip on you anymore. That's the sort of lesson you an' your kind understand. But I reckon I'm too soft for my own good. So I'll do this by the book an' hope you learn something from it anyhow. Mind, though. If you go an' disappoint me I won't have much choice but to put a bullet in your belly. You hear me?"

"Yeah."

"What?"

"Yes, sir."

It was what they taught them when they were inside. The Man was always Sir. Every con knew that.

"Yes, sir," this con docilely repeated.

"That's fine then. Bring your other hand behind you. That's right. Now hold it there. That's fine, thank you." Longarm cuffed the stupid SOB's hands behind his back and told the bartender, "Don't let anything happen till I get back, hear?"

Then he led his prisoner out of the saloon and up the canyon toward Harry Bolt's Cargyle jail. Not that Longarm wanted to owe Harry any favors, but his was the only jail around. He had no choice but to lodge his man there until he could make arrangements to have the poor sonuvabitch hauled up to Denver so he could be charged and tried for assault on a federal officer.

Chapter 24

If the crowd Longarm drew had been willing to drink while they watched, Clete Terry would forever have been in Longarm's debt. But for some unspoken yet almost inviolable reason the men who gathered in the saloon were somber, quiet, and nearly completely dry.

Longarm doubted the place sold two dollars worth of beer and liquor that evening, and the gambling tables were empty. The whores stayed out of sight too, and presumably had the night off to spend with their families. Or off somewhere sulking about the lack of income if they had no families in town.

The night bartender—there was no sign of Terry himself—tried to limit the free dinner spread to those who bought and paid for at least one beer. Even that was not enough to promote the sale of any beer. Nor, for that matter, to curb the appetites of those who wanted to help themselves to the free food. The bartender eventually solved his problem by taking the free dinner away and posting a hand-lettered sign offering a beer and sandwich for ten cents. Longarm didn't see any takers for that deal, which everyone was used to getting anyway for the nickel price of the beer.

"You know, mister, things sure were better around here

before you came along," the bartender told Longarm at one point, a note of exasperation plain in his voice.

"I got no problem with you, friend. You go right ahead an' do whatever you generally do."

"Mister, I'm generally busy selling beer."

"I wish I could help you. I truly do."

"You could go away."

Longarm sighed. "Your boss knows what this is about."

"Look, maybe I can talk to him."

"Go ahead."

"If you'd just tell me what it is you want . . ."

"Restitution," Longarm said.

"Pardon me?"

"The word is—"

"Oh, I know the word. I just don't understand you using it in connection with this here. Whatever has Clete done that you're wanting him to make restitution?"

"He knows. I'm sure he'll understand if you tell him what I've said."

"Mister, I'd be willing to memorize a bunch of nonsense from you if that would get things back to normal."

"Then all you need to tell him is that one word, friend. Restitution. He can take it from there if he wants."

"I'll sure try it." The bartender looked indecisive for a moment, then shrugged. "What the hell. He said I was to take charge." The fellow raised his voice and called out, "We're closing again, boys. Everybody go on now. We're shutting down for the night."

It wasn't yet eight o'clock.

Longarm waited until everyone else was out, then stood outside and watched while the place was closed down and locked.

He would check again later, of course, to make sure they didn't reopen once he was gone.

What he was figuring, though, was that Clete Terry was a

man who couldn't stand to lose money too many days in a row. And for the time being he would be spending more to keep his saloon afloat than he was taking in from the few paying customers.

Before very long, Longarm figured, Terry would be wanting to reach an accommodation. Or square off in a last-ditch fight. One or the other.

The truth was that Longarm didn't much give a shit which way Cletus Terry decided to go.

He left the dark and silent saloon behind and went to see about a dinner for three that he could carry back to the Fulton house.

Chapter 25

Longarm was proud of himself. Angela had had Buddy change the sheets on her bed this afternoon, and Longarm had been able to get all the way through the meal without slopping any broth, clabber, or honey-sweetened tea onto the clean bedding. He considered that an accomplishment of the first water.

"You look a lot better this evening," he said as he piled the dirty dishes onto the tray he'd brought from the cafe.

"You're just saying that," Angela protested. "I'm sure I look a perfect sight."

He grinned. "If you're feeling up to fishin' for compliments, ma'am, then I reckon you're on the mend for certain sure."

"Compliments? Why, I intended no such thing."

"Huh. So you say. But I been around a while, y'know. An' any time a pretty lady goes to mentioning how bad she looks, it's for sure she wants a gentleman to correct that statement by telling her how *good* she looks. Mind you remember that, Buddy. It's a truth every man should oughta know."

The boy grinned. Angela tried to, but ended up wincing as the expression pulled at the corners of her mouth where her scabs were still mighty tender.

"I can take them dishes back, Mr. Long," Buddy offered.

"Those dishes," his mother corrected.

"Yes'm."

"Thanks for the offer, son, but I have to go right past there anyway."

"Could I help you carry them then? I'm strong, you know. I can help."

"All right. That sounds fair." Longarm figured the boy probably wanted to help pull his weight. Possibly his mama had spoken to him about that before Longarm returned that evening. Whatever, there was no reason why he couldn't carry some of the stuff if he wanted to. "That all right with you, Miz Fulton? I'll send him right back in case you need anything before I come in for the night."

"I'm fine here. Really."

"Good. Buddy, you can go ahead an' gather up the rest of the things. I'll take the tray an' you can carry that pail there."

Not the least bit shy about the open display of affection, Buddy kissed his mother good-bye, then he and Longarm took the soiled containers and whatnot that Longarm had brought from the cafe, carrying them out into the young night.

It wasn't late, but the night air was cool and pleasant. The sky was cloudless, and the stars were as brilliant as far-off gas lamps overhead. Longarm noticed the stars, but Buddy paid them no mind.

"Mr. Long?"

"Yes, son?"

"Do you like my ma?"

"Yes, I do, Buddy. Quite a lot."

"She likes you too, you know. She told me she does."

Longarm smiled. He shifted the tray he was carrying into the crook of one arm so he'd have a hand free, then reached over and tousled the boy's hair so as to take any sting away from what he had to say. He could see what was coming— which explained why Buddy'd been so eager to help carry the dinner stuff this evening—and wanted to head it off before the youngster got to counting on things that wouldn't ever happen.

"I like your mama a lot, Buddy. But there's something I want you to know. The way I like her—and for that matter the way she likes me too, I'm sure—it ain't the same kind of liking that a man and a woman have for each other when they go to getting married."

"Oh."

"The way I like your mama, and her back to me, is the kind of liking real good friends have for each other. Where we want good things for the other person an' will do whatever we can to help see that that's so. But not where we'd want to live together forever and ever as man an' wife. You understand?"

"Kinda like me and Peppy?" the boy suggested.

Longarm smiled. "That ain't exactly how I'd've thought to put it. But I suppose you could say that it's kinda that way. Nice an' friendly but not . . . you know."

"No, sir, I don't know. Not if you're talking about the stuff grown men do with women." He made a sour face. "That damn Rick, he says men put their pizzles in girls' poop holes and pee inside there. Is that true, Mr. Long?"

Longarm laughed. He probably shouldn't have, but he couldn't help it. He ruffled Buddy's hair again and said, "No, son, that isn't even close to being true. An' if I can make a suggestion, don't pay too much attention to what all Rick tells you in the future. That boy don't know half as much as he thinks he does."

Buddy looked mighty relieved to hear that from a grown-up he obviously had come to trust.

"That's good, Mr. Long. But I think—"

Longarm never would know what Buddy thought.

The night was illuminated by a sheet of yellow flame that blossomed across the street to their right, and the peaceful quiet of the evening was shattered by the bellowing roar of a shotgun blast.

Little Buddy, walking between Longarm and the gun, cried out and lurched sideways, stumbling into Longarm and knocking Longarm's gun arm askew before the boy fell to the ground.

Bowls, dishes, and small containers crashed to the ground as tray and pail alike were abandoned in midair, and with a flash of rage every bit as quick and every bit as deadly as that shotgun blast had been, Longarm clawed his Colt from his holster and dropped flat an instant before the second shotshell charge exploded from the mouth of an alley.

Chapter 26

As Longarm hit the ground he fired two quick shots about belt level in the direction the shotgun blasts had come from, and then quickly rolled to the side.

He was half blinded by the bright muzzle flashes. But so was the other guy, he figured.

A third gunshot came from the alley mouth, this one a much smaller flare of fire and a much lighter, sharper report. A revolver that would be, or a very small-caliber rifle. The flash came from the opposite side of the alley, not where the shotgun had been. So either the man with the empty shotgun had moved to avoid Longarm's return fire, or there were two of them over there doing the shooting.

Longarm had no idea who was there or how many, but he saw no reason to take any chances.

He triggered the big Colt again, one shot into the side of the alley where the small-caliber weapon had just fired, and another into the black, empty space where the shotgun had been moments earlier.

He would have appreciated a scream or maybe the sound of a body falling to the earth, but all he got was silence.

Nearby little Buddy had begun to cry. Longarm hated that. But he sure as hell couldn't take time out to comfort a kid or tend to his wounds, no matter what.

Longarm rolled again to get away from gunfire directed toward his muzzle flashes, then quickly shucked the empty brass from his revolver and thumbed fresh cartridges into the cylinder.

He blinked, trying to hurry the return of his night vision.

Well before he'd had time enough to begin to see properly again he was on his feet and, bent low to the ground, darted crab-like across the street, moving swiftly from one side to the other while he ran toward the alley where those shots had originated.

He reached the corner of the building there and stopped to listen.

There was no sound of ragged breathing—damn few men are cold enough to be able to shoot at someone from ambush without getting worked up about it—but from somewhere deep in the alley he could hear footsteps retreating.

It was a gamble. Those footsteps could be the gunman. Or it could be one of a pair of gunmen while the other waited for Longarm to silhouette himself against the alley mouth. Or shit, the guy at the back of the alley could be some innocent drunk who'd been awakened by the commotion and was trying to get away now while the ambusher, with or without a friend to back him, waited for another shot.

A gamble, all right. If Longarm guessed wrong he could wind up dead. Or else let the attacker get away.

Neither of those possibilities very much appealed to him.

Scowling, he took a fresh grip on the Colt, braced himself, and then with a loud roar calculated to startle any remaining ambusher launched himself around the corner and into the alley.

He was greeted by . . . nothing at all.

The goddamn alley was empty.

The gunman, or gunmen, had gotten clean away.

Longarm took only a few scant seconds to investigate the trash-strewn corridor that contained a stray cat but no other living thing.

Then he turned and ran back to Buddy's side.

"Y'know," Longarm reflected, "this here house could end up bein' designated as Cargyle's new hospital if this keeps up." He winked at Buddy and, out of the boy's sight, gave the kid's mama a reassuring squeeze on the shoulder.

Buddy was propped up on his bed with feather pillows behind and the family's extra-best-for-company quilt spread over him. He had a plate of cookies on one side of him and a glass of sarsaparilla soda on the other.

He looked, in fact, pretty damn chipper.

The truth was that he'd barely been scratched by a couple of the shotgun pellets, just enough to sting like hell and draw some blood, and now he was making the most of it.

By tomorrow noon, Longarm figured, Buddy Fulton would be the number-one hero among the boys of Cargyle, Colorado.

Why, any kid who actually got himself shot in a gunfight, and lived to tell about it, would be the awe and the envy of every other kid for miles and miles around.

He'd have bragging rights for years to come.

And with luck a scar or two to show off whenever the subject came up.

One pellet had sliced across the boy's right cheek. Another had pinked his upper arm just below the shoulder. A couple more had ripped up his shirt some without doing any harm—although those had sure turned that shirt into a trophy to be fingered and passed around while all the boyish talk was taking place—and a final pellet had hit square in the side of the boy's head just above his right ear. That one could have been deadly if the range had been just a little shorter, the powder charge just a little heavier, or the size of the pellet itself just a little larger.

That one was the only piece of shot Longarm had been able to recover, but it was enough to show him that the shells in the shotgun had been filled with a load suitable for the hunting of ducks, not men.

Longarm judged the shot to be about a number-four size. Good for ducks or foxes but too light for geese . . . or humans. Birdshot fired from across the street like that Buddy would hardly have been bothered by. Buckshot striking him in the same places would have killed him. All in all the kid could count himself plenty lucky. This way he had all the bravado but damn little of the pain that could've come his way.

Longarm made sure Buddy was comfortable—comfortable? hell, he was in his glory—then insisted on helping Angela back into her bed.

Buddy's mother, quite naturally, had been much more worried about her son than herself. Now, though, with Buddy safely cleaned up, bandaged, and put to bed, she was commencing to look used up. The excitement was too much for a woman with all the healing she still had to do.

"Come along now."

"But—"

"No, I insist. Really. C'mon now." Longarm took her by the elbow and tugged and prodded until he got her turned the right way, then poked and hauled on her again until she started moving. "I swear, woman, I've had less trouble herding *ladrónes.*"

"Ladrónes?"

"Cattle that've gone back to the brush an' turned wild. Now quit hanging back on me an' get yourself inta that bed before I . . . well, I don't know what I'll do if I have to. But I'll think of something that you won't like."

"All right. I'll be good." She gave him an impish look—not so easy to do with a face that was mostly purple and black— and looked like she was about to say or do something to test his threat.

Just as quickly she became serious. "Mr. Long . . . I can't tell you how much I appreciate what you've done for Eric. If it hadn't been for you . . ."

"Angela—excuse me, I mean Miz Fulton—the truth is, if it hadn't been for me, there wouldn't nothing have happened to Buddy. Whoever that was in the alley was shooting at me, not at your son."

"I know that is true but . . . you've been so kind to both of us. So decent. I only wish there was something I could do to repay you for . . . everything."

Lightly, and very gently, he touched her battered cheek and used the ball of his thumb to wipe away the drop of moisture that was beginning to collect and shimmer in the corner of her eye. "I'm the one owes you. Not the other way round."

She shook her head right vigorously to deny that statement.

"Well, we ain't gonna fight about it. Now you get back in that bed there. I'm gonna go out again, but I won't be long."

"Where—?"

"Me an' Buddy never got those dishes back to the cafe, for one thing," he said with a smile. "I'll gather those up, whatever's left of 'em, and take 'em back. Though I don't expect much. When that gun went off, me an' Buddy wasn't thinking about taking care of no dishes, let me tell you. I think the sound of breaking crockery was louder than the shooting for those first few seconds." He chuckled and winked at her. "And I still gotta check an' see if that saloon is closed up. That's what I went out for to begin with, actually, but never got 'er done. Figured while I was out too I oughta go up an' tell Chief Bolt about the murder attempt in his town. Not that it'll do any good, but this way everything will've been done by the book. There can't be no comeback against me for not following the rules an' keeping the local law informed of what I'm doing in their town."

Angela nodded. "You'll be careful, won't you?"

He touched her cheek again. "I'll be careful." He didn't mention that, if it was up to him, he'd as soon that son of a bitch in the shadows made another try. Particularly if he was going to use duckshot in the gun. Longarm would thoroughly approve of getting another crack at the guy.

He left Angela in her draped-off bedroom area, and gave Buddy a grin and a chuck under the chin, then let himself out into the night again.

By the time his boot heel hit the plank that was laid at the front doorway for a stoop, Longarm's expression was grim and his gun hand poised in readiness.

Chapter 27

There sure as hell wasn't much worth taking back to the cafe where they'd made up the supper. He gathered up what he could, though, and returned it along with payment for the broken stuff.

He also borrowed a lantern from the man who ran the cafe and took another, better look in the alley where the guy with the shotgun had hidden.

Longarm found exactly what he expected to see there. Not a damn thing.

As he was walking back to the cafe to return the lantern, it occurred to him that the shotgunner couldn't have been waiting there in ambush. Not deliberately, because Longarm himself hadn't known he would pass that way. It wasn't something he'd planned on ahead of time, just something that happened after supper.

So the gunman must have seen him coming and taken advantage of an opportunity. The son of a bitch!

Longarm was especially pissed because the man had risked killing a kid in his eagerness to get Longarm.

It wasn't like he considered U.S. deputy marshals to be fair game. But there was something especially reprehensible about any man who would shoot with a young'un in the line of fire.

It took someone who was really sick or really determined to fire under those conditions.

And Longarm had no idea, none, who in Cargyle might carry that virulent a hatred for him.

It was something to think about, he reflected.

He returned the lantern to the cafe owner, then drifted past Clete Terry's saloon. The place was dark and shuttered, the padlock still in place on the front door.

Good. Longarm wasn't forgetting about that SOB and what he'd done to Angela Fulton.

One way or another, he was determined, Terry was going to pay restitution. In full, by damn.

As he walked into the canyon and onto company land, he wondered if Cletus Terry might be the motivating force behind the shooting tonight.

It was possible, of course. When you are dealing with incomprehensible, impossible, illogical—and sometimes just plain crazy as hell—human beings, there are no guarantees. Some people will do just damn near anything.

Even so, Longarm didn't much like Terry as a suspect in this thing.

It seemed simply . . . too much.

There wasn't that much at stake here, after all. A few hundred bucks' restitution. That was what Longarm had in mind. That and a public apology. Was that worth killing for? More to the point, was that worth dying for? Cletus Terry was an idiot. But surely he wasn't *that* big a fool.

Of course Longarm could be wrong about that, he conceded. But his gut reaction was that he shouldn't blame this on Clete Terry. Not without some pretty good evidence to the contrary.

Which left him with . . . shit, that's what it left him with.

He kinda wished Terry was the man behind the gun. At least that would be quick and clean and soon done with.

In the meantime . . .

"You again," Longarm observed with a grin.

The coal miner shrugged and grinned back. "Do a fella a favor, willya, mate? Gimme a drink of water, eh?" It was the same prisoner Longarm had seen in here two days earlier. The man looked like he hadn't changed so much as his socks in that time. Certainly he hadn't bathed. Or, apparently, learned anything.

"I'm looking for Chief Bolt," Longarm said.

"Still?"

"Again."

The prisoner shrugged. "Look, are you gonna be a pal and give me a dipper of water or not?"

"Sure," Longarm said, relenting this time if only because the cantankerous so-and-so hadn't been willing to spill any information before unless Longarm showed cooperation first.

"There's a bucket behind the desk there. And while you're right there anyhow—"

"I know. Your tobacco box is in the drawer."

The prisoner beamed. "You remember."

"You're a hard man to forget. Though I expect I can manage if I set my mind to it."

The man laughed. And cheerfully accepted both the metal dipper of tepid water Longarm handed him and the twist of tobacco.

"I believe you were saying something about Harry Bolt?"

"Uh-huh. He's in town. Likely over at that saloon he owns."

"Which one would that be?"

The miner frowned in thoughtful concentration. "Y'know," he said after a moment, "if it has a name I don't b'lieve I've ever heard what it is. It's the biggest down there anyhow. Guy name of Terry runs it for him. Clete Terry."

Longarm rolled his eyes. Son of a bitch! Clete Terry was a hired hand. And for that asshole Harry Bolt at that. Shee-it! Double shee-it. With honey and walnuts on top.

"You don't happen to know if there's living quarters or anything of the like in the back of that saloon, do you?"

"You're right, mister. I wouldn't happen to know that. But there's rooms for the girls to use. I wouldn't know about the private parts of the place."

"No, I don't suppose you would. Look, thanks for the help."

"Anytime." The prisoner grinned. "I'm in residence fairly often."

"Yeah, so I gathered." Longarm touched the brim of his hat and turned to leave.

He was halfway out the door before something occurred to him, and he turned back inside the Cargyle jail.

"Say, friend."

"Umm?"

"Where's the other prisoner that's supposed to be here tonight?"

"That fella with the short hair and the rock-pile sunburn?"

"That's the one."

"Bolt turned him loose right after supper."

"What!" That man was a federal prisoner, dammit. Longarm's, to be exact. Harry Bolt had no damn right to spring him.

The coal miner certainly saw nothing exceptional about it. Nor would he have any reason to lie. "Bolt opened the cage on him just a little while after I got here. Which I want to tell you was before supper this time. I'm not making that mistake again, thank you. Damn Bolt won't feed a hungry man if it isn't on the stroke of his stinking clock."

A protest that rose in Longarm's throat was stillborn. After all, it would do no good to squawk and protest to this fella.

Only to Harry Bolt. And of course to the ex-con. Damn them both.

He was on his way out the door again when once more a stray thought clutched at his coattails and called him back inside the jail.

"Say, friend."

"Yeah?"

"This man Harry turned loose. Do you remember what kind of gear he had with him?"

"The clothes on his back, some loose change that I seen Bolt give him out of that drawer there, and a belly gun. Long, thin-looking thing, but I wouldn't know what kind it was. I can't say as I know much about guns and stuff like that."

"Yeah, well, thanks, neighbor. Thanks a lot."

"Stop by anytime. I'm always glad for the company."

Longarm touched the brim of his hat again, and this time made it all the way outside and down the road toward town without remembering some reason to go back.

Chapter 28

If Clete Terry or Harry Bolt lived at Bolt's saloon, Longarm couldn't see or hear them inside. The place looked completely closed up and empty. Both men had to live *someplace*, of course. Even a sidewinder has to have a hole to crawl into. But no one Longarm talked to seemed to know where Terry or Bolt crawled in at night.

They didn't know or wouldn't tell, that is. After all, it was pretty plain to folks around Cargyle by now that this visitor and their local police chief were on a collision course. And siding with the local law was simple prudence the way Longarm saw it. It wasn't anything he would go and hold against anyone.

Still, it put a crimp in his wire. There were things he damn sure wanted to ask Harry Bolt about.

Starting with just why in hell that ex-convict was walking the streets tonight—or more likely rattling down the railroad tracks miles and miles away by now—when Longarm had put him in jail as a federal prisoner.

Bolt knew better than that. Any wet-behind-the-ears night constable would know better. And Harry Bolt, asshole though he undoubtedly was, had been around for a long time.

No, something was definitely happening here that didn't set

any too well in the gullet. Something that wasn't at all the way it oughta be.

Still, until he could catch up with Harry Bolt and commence getting some answers, there wasn't much he could do to unravel the puzzle. He stopped by one of the smaller, and filthier, of the town's saloons for a nighttime knock, then headed back to the Fulton place. He was more alert than usual in case his pal with the shotgun wanted another dance, but this time there was no excitement to keep him awake. He bolted the door shut as quiet as he could and crawled into the blankets laid out on his pallet by the stove.

There wasn't any red glow coming from the stove this time. No fire had been lighted there since yesterday as far as he knew.

But there was sound.

A thump. A bump. A muffled, heartfelt curse.

Which answered that for certain sure. It wasn't Buddy getting up to head for the outhouse that he was hearing. It was Buddy's mama moving around again.

My, but that little ol' woman had a mouth on her when she wanted to turn loose of it. She must have been taking lessons from a mule skinner. Maybe from a whole passel of them.

Longarm lay there and grinned into the darkness.

He heard another thump as she walked into the edge of the kitchen table, then the scraping of wood on wood as she bumped into a chair and sent it skidding across the floor.

Longarm did the decent thing. He felt around on the floor until he found the cheroots and sulfur-tipped matches he'd laid out there earlier, and struck one of the matches so Angela could see her way to wherever she was going. It was either that, he figured, or Buddy was gonna be wide awake from all the commotion she was causing.

She wasn't going to the outhouse, he quickly concluded. She was barefoot and wearing nothing but her flimsy nightdress.

The robe that he'd so carefully laid where she could reach it was nowhere to be seen.

"Thanks," she whispered, giving the offending chair a rueful look and going wide around it. Having bumped it once, she'd been pointed straight at it a second time.

"Anytime." He held the match while Angela glanced once in the direction of Buddy's cot—the boy's breathing was deep and regular; he was sleeping so hard he was damn near unconscious—then opened the top of her nightdress and let the cloth slither down her body to fall in a cotton puddle at her feet.

This was the first time Longarm had seen Angela naked. She wasn't at all bad. A mite on the skinny side, but her tits were more than a mouthful and her mound was plump and proud. She had a flat belly and slender thighs. Her ribs stood out all plain to see like the bars of one of those . . . the word wouldn't come to him just then—that musical instrument they played with little hammers and danced all around between acts at the hurdy-gurdy theater shows. He frowned. Then the furrows in his brow eased. Xylophone. That was what the sons of bitches were called. Anyway, that was kind of what Angela's ribs looked like.

It occurred to him that she'd gone and taken off the wrapping that had been tied so tight around her to protect those broken ribs the barber said she had. He supposed she must have had her reasons. Like probably not being able to breathe. He'd been wrapped up like that a time or two himself and knew how just plain miserable that cure can be.

"Are you all right?" he asked.

"Isn't that kind of a silly question at the moment?" she responded.

"Yeah, I s'pose it is." The match burned down to his fingers, and he shook it out quick before his fingernail caught fire.

"Hush now. We don't want to wake Eric."

"We?"

"Shhh. You're going to make me laugh, and I don't want to do that. It hurts."

"Sorry. So, um, what was it that you wanted to do if it ain't tell jokes an' play pinochle?"

"What makes you think I don't want to play pinochle?"

"You'd 'a brought a lamp."

"Actually I did want to play pinochle. But I forgot the lamp. Do you think we can think of something else instead?" Her hand was groping around in the dark. This time it wasn't a chair she was feeling for, though. It wasn't a chair she was finding either, although the particular part of Longarm's anatomy that she settled on to explore in more detail was soon about as hard as the leg of a chair. "Oh, my," she whispered. "I do like this."

"You sure you're feelin' up to this?"

"I am. So are you."

"Look, Angela, you don't owe me a damn thing. An' I wouldn't want to hurt you. So whyn't you slip back inta bed now before—"

"Shhh." She squeezed his cock with one hand, and with the other laid a finger over his lips to hush him. "I'd shut you up with a kiss, except it would hurt too much to bend over like that. Do you mind?"

"I ain't complaining."

"Good. Now hold still and let me do this. Otherwise I'm afraid we'd get to thrashing around, and I don't think I could stand much of that just now."

"I'll try an' be good," he promised, only half facetiously.

"As I recall, sir, you are very good indeed."

Longarm chuckled. And offered no objections when Angela squatted over him with one foot planted tight against each side of him just slightly above waist level.

She touched him lightly on the flat of his chest with one hand to stabilize her balance, and with the other guided his cock while she lowered herself onto his manhood.

Angela needed no preparation. She was wet and ready before the head of his cock ever slid in between the lips of her pussy.

He heard her sigh softly in the darkness as the length of him burrowed deeper and ever deeper inside until she had captured all of him within her.

"Nice," she whispered. "So nice."

"What, did you come here to talk the night away?" he teased.

She laughed, a little too loudly, then continued to laugh under her breath. He could feel the tiny movements and pulsations as her stomach quivered and rippled with the laughter. It was a nice feeling. Friendly, sort of. He liked it. And told her so.

"Thank you." Slowly, stroking long and deep, she lifted herself over him and then came down again. Gently. Deeply.

"Damn but that's nice."

"I do agree, sir, and I do be thanking you." She leaned forward and touched his cheek with a fond caress.

Yeah, Longarm thought, Buddy Fulton's mama was one nice little lady. Sweet and giving. And a good screw too. Never mind what she looked like in the daytime after Cletus Terry got done beating on her. She was one very nice little woman.

Longarm lay back and let her gently draw the juices of his masculinity out of his body and into hers.

He came with a sigh and a shuddering, pulsing flow, then closed his eyes and let sleep claim him. He didn't even know when Angela left him. And if she bumped into any furniture on her way back to bed, well, this time she didn't wake him.

Chapter 29

"Dang it, Miz Fulton, you're in no condition to be lifting that heavy griddle. An' believe me, you an' Buddy don't want to try eating what I'd cook. So you stay right there where you can get on with the business of mending while I go down to the cafe and fetch us back something. No, I ain't gonna listen to no mumbling or fussing about this. My mind is made up on the subject."

"If you insist."

"I do."

"In that case, Mr. Long, could I ask you for some tea today?"

"You don't like coffee?"

"Not really."

He'd been bringing coffee right along and had never thought to ask if she liked it. Hell, everybody liked coffee, right? Well, almost everybody. So tea it would be today. And coffee. The thought of starting the day with a dainty little old cup of dishwater tea instead of a good stout mug of coffee was too awful to contemplate.

"I'll bring you some tea. What about you, Buddy?"

"Could I have a pork chop?"

"You can have as many of 'em as you like. What'll it be?"

The boy's eyes became wide with the prospect. Pork chops? As many as he liked? "Two pork chops?"

"Three if you'd ruther. It don't make no nevermind to me, son."

Buddy grinned. "Three pork chops then. And some fried taters. And some hominy. I love hominy. And some—"

"Eric!" his mother warned.

"It's all right, Miz Fulton. He can have anything he wants. I said so. Only thing is, whatever he takes, that's what he's gotta finish. I won't be carrying the stuff up here just for him to waste."

Angela subsided. So did Buddy's enthusiasm. "I have to clean my plate?"

"Darn right you do."

"Then maybe you should make it two pork chops. And not so much taters and hominy. What do you think?"

"I think you're gonna have you a good breakfast. Miz Fulton, how 'bout you?"

Her request was considerably more modest than her son's had been. Tea, toast, maybe a little jam if it wasn't too much trouble.

He'd just order up three hearty breakfasts, Longarm figured, and Angela and Buddy could work out between them who got around what.

He made a mental note of what he needed, then picked up his Stetson and unbolted the shanty door.

The door hadn't more than swung open before there was the booming report of a shotgun blast, and the door kicked back on its hinges under the thundering impact of the shotgun charge.

Sometime since last night, Longarm thought even as he was swinging into action, the guy with the two-shot gun had gone and gotten himself some real shotgun shells. He wasn't loaded for duck hunting this morning.

143

"Lower. No, scoot back just a little bit. That's better." Longarm's first concern was for Angela and Buddy. He had the both of them lying on his pallet with the protective bulk of the iron stove between them and the shotgun outside. A heavy shotshell pellet fired at close range can punch clean through the sort of thin lathing that the Fulton shanty was made from, and he didn't want either one of these innocents hurt any further on his account.

He put them in the safest place he could find inside the house, then dragged the wood box over to shield them from the side. He stuffed a pillow underneath the stove to more or less close in the gap between the iron legs, then covered the woman and the boy with the quilt he'd slept under. A good quilt can stop a partly spent shotgun pellet. Maybe. Often enough to be worth the effort now anyway.

"Both of you lay still. I don't wanta have to think about what my target is. If I see something move I wanta know I'm free to fire. Do you understand that? It ain't a matter of who's brave or who ain't. It's a matter of can I shoot without worrying about you two. An' that can be the difference between me living or me dying. I ain't being a hero 'bout this. I'm bein' selfish. An' I wanta stay living so I can keep right on bein' that way. You understand that. Buddy? Miz Fulton?"

He waited until he got a nod of understanding from each of them, then draped the quilt over on top of them, covering even their heads so as to give them as much protection as was possible.

"Wait here an' don't move. I'll be back quick as I can be, but I don't know how long that's gonna be an' won't make you no promises that I might not be able to keep. Just you both mind, you stay here till I come fetch you. That way we'll all be safe."

He touched Angela on the shoulder and gave Buddy a poke

on the upper arm, then palmed his Colt and eased up beside the open doorway.

The door itself had been torn up pretty good by the shotgun blast. The thing was definitely in need of repairs.

Better a slab of gray, weathered wood than Custis Long's belly, though. Doors would be easier to replace.

He stood there for a moment and looked around the room. He saw what he wanted and, keeping well back from the door frame, made his way across the room to fetch it.

At the least, he figured, Angela's robe was going to need laundering when this thing was over with.

Well, he'd pay for the washing. The point was to be alive so he could pay.

He held his .44 ready in one hand, and with the other shook the robe out so it dangled full length to the floor. Then, with a sweep of his arm, he floated the dark green robe out the door. The garment sailed out like a ghost riding on a breeze.

The shotgun boomed again, and Longarm burst through the doorway at full speed.

One charge of pellets smacked into the wall of the house just before Longarm flew out. Another punched into the wood just behind him as the gunman reacted without taking time for careful aim.

With both barrels expended Longarm was free to look for cover. Otherwise he'd have had to hit the ground and hope he could keep ahead of the shotgunner's swinging muzzles.

He trampled clean over Angela's fluttering robe and legged it around the corner of the shack long before the ambusher would have had time to reload.

He ducked into a crouch and squeezed in between Peppy's lean-to shelter and the back of the house. He still hadn't had a chance to see where it was the shotgunner was hiding. And he didn't want that information to come as any surprise when he did figure it out. Better to be cautious now even when he thought the shotgunner should be out of sight.

The Fulton place was one of a handful of similar shacks that had been built without pattern along the banks of the sluggish creek that passed through the Cargyle canyon. Longarm slipped around to the back of the place next door, and eased forward along its side wall until he could peer around the front corner and look for the shotgunner.

There wasn't much to see. Another small clutch of shacks on the far side of the railroad tracks. A well with a rock wall around it and a windlass and bucket mounted overhead. An abandoned wagon box with weeds growing out of it. Peppy's cart beside the Fulton place—Longarm had just run right by that cart without so much as noticing it was there—and across the way a trash heap that seemed to consist mostly of broken whiskey bottles.

There was no sign of the man with the shotgun.

The guy might well have given up and run away by now. He'd done that last night. But then it is easier to get away from someone at night. In broad daylight he might figure he was committed and would have to stick through this to the end.

Longarm concentrated on examining every detail within his line of sight, no matter how insignificant it might seem at the moment.

He let his unconscious mind work on that while at a conscious level he thought through what little he knew or could assume here.

For one thing, this time it hadn't been any accident that the gunman ran into him.

This time the SOB had been lying in wait outside the Fulton house. This time the guy knew perfectly good and well where he could expect Longarm to appear come morning. The fact that there was only one door leading in or out had made it ridiculously easy for him.

So this time there was no possibility that it was an impulse sort of thing. It wasn't some guilt-ridden fugitive seeing a fcdcral deputy approach and wrongly concluding that because Longarm was there Longarm just had to be after him. That sort of thing happened fairly often. But not this time.

No, this time it was cold, it was deliberate, and it was premeditated.

This time if Longarm took the man alive, there was a good chance he would hang for his trouble.

Longarm wondered if the shotgunner knew that. Probably. And if he did, then—

That wagon box. An intuitive jolt leaped from Longarm's unconscious into the forefront of his thoughts. In the wagon box across the road there were weeds growing high at the back of the box and all along two of the other sides. But along the near side and toward the front, up toward where there was a gap in the old and broken side boards, there were no weeds. Why? Was there some good reason why weeds would be growing everywhere else inside that wagon box except there? Or had weeds been growing there, and now were they being crushed to the earth by the presence of a body lying atop them?

There probably could be fifty perfectly good reasons why a weed wouldn't want to grow on that spot over there.

Longarm didn't believe a one of them.

His bet was that he'd found his gunman.

And while shotgun pellets will often break through lathing, so will .44 slugs punch through old planking.

Not always, but sometimes.

And hell, .44 cartridges are cheap. A lot cheaper than blood.

Longarm reached into his pocket and got a handful of loose cartridges in his left hand, then triggered two shots into the seemingly empty wagon box, aiming his first shots carefully into the gap toward the front where he thought those shotgun blasts might've come from.

He fired twice and reloaded, fired twice more and quickly reloaded, fired twice again and started to reload.

Six shots. If the shotgunner thought he was empty . . .

A figure popped into view as abruptly as one of those spring-loaded jack-in-the-box things jumping out at a child.

Longarm flattened himself against the side of the house where he was standing. A spray of buckshot splintered the dried-out wood, stinging Longarm's wrist but doing no harm.

The sonuvabitch was quick. Lordy, he was quick. He had fired and was skeedaddling for cover about as quick as a man could blink.

Longarm snapped a shot at him, but couldn't tell if he'd connected or not.

The shotgunner reached the protection of one of the houses across the way, and swung around to throw another load of buck toward Longarm.

Longarm had no idea where that blast went, but it wasn't close enough to worry about.

The scattergun was empty now. But it wouldn't stay that way more than a few seconds. Longarm took advantage of the time he had and dashed across the road and over the railroad tracks.

Too long. It was taking him too long, and he was exposed and vulnerable. Some inner sense or timing sent up a warning flag, and he dropped to the ground, rolling, an instant before the reloaded shotgun roared. A bee swarm of lead pellets cut through the air above him, and he scrambled on all fours for the cover of the trash mound.

Another blast from the shotgun sent shards of glass cascading through the air like a rainstorm of diamonds.

The SOB had plenty of shells with him today, Longarm reflected. And plenty of determination too.

Well, he was sensible to go at it that way, everything considered. For Longarm had recognized him by now. It was that miserable little shit of an ex-con who'd braced Longarm in the saloon yesterday. And who'd been let out of jail last evening, dammit.

If Longarm could've reached Harry Bolt's throat right then, he would have strangled the shithead. And that just to get his attention. After that, by damn, he'd hurt the idjit.

So far Longarm didn't know the little bastard's name. But it wouldn't be so hard to figure out. A talk with the warden up at Canon City would probably clear that up. And it didn't really matter who the guy was anyway. The point was that Longarm knew him. There was no backing down for the ex-con now. He was committed to this until either he or Longarm lay dead on the ground.

Longarm braced himself, then burst onto his feet with the Colt barking in his fist.

Chapter 30

Longarm's third shot, hastily thrown—but not wildly; there was a difference—ripped into the shotgunner's elbow, slamming his arm backward and dragging the aim of the shotgun with it so that the charge of deadly buckshot intended for Longarm went harmlessly wide.

The scattergun was too heavy and cumbersome for the man to manage one-handed. He tried, but quickly realized the futility of the attempt and threw the gun down. His right elbow shattered and his right arm useless, he clawed for the Navy Colt with his left hand.

"Stop, dammit. You don't got a chance," Longarm shouted.

The ex-con was solid grit. Longarm didn't particularly admire that in the son of a bitch. But he sure had to admit it was there. The man dragged iron left-handed and fumbled to draw the hammer back.

"Drop it right now or I shoot," Longarm warned.

The man managed to cock the revolver and shakily tried to take aim.

"I mean it. No more chances."

The man stared over his sights into Longarm's cold eyes. He had no choice, dammit. He really had no choice. Longarm fired a fourth round and a fifth. His sixth and final cartridge was unnecessary. The fourth impacted square on the ex-con's breastbone, driving lead and splinters of bone into his racing heart. The fifth shot took him in the side of the neck, severing the big artery there and sending a bright spray of blood briefly into the air until the sudden loss of pressure slowed the flow to a trickle. By then it didn't matter anyway. By then the man was face-down in the blood-soaked dirt, his eyes glazing and his limbs twitching and jerking in random spasms while his bowels and kidneys emptied. The stench of his shit mingled with the copper odor of the blood to form the peculiarly ugly stink of sudden death.

Longarm stood upright, weary now despite the early hour, and by long habit reloaded his Colt before he walked cautiously forward to make damn sure this man would no longer be gunning for him.

Before he had time to reach the body, doors began opening all around, and within seconds there was an inquisitive crowd beginning to grow. Longarm for the most part ignored them. He had little but contempt for the mindless assholes who were drawn to the sight of another man's blood.

"You. Boy."

"Yes, sir?"

"Rick, isn't it?"

The boy acted like he wasn't sure if he should be pleased that this deadly visitor remembered him or not. He swallowed hard and nodded.

"D'you still have that wagon?"

"I can get it."

"Do that, boy. I want to hire you to haul something for me."

"Yes, sir. Right away."

Rick hurried off, and Longarm shouldered through the crowd of people without acknowledging any of them.

He knelt beside the body, careful to keep from getting any of the bright scarlet blood on his pants legs, and checked through the dead man's pockets.

Interesting, he thought. Damned interesting.

When he'd booked this man into Harry Bolt's jail yesterday afternoon the fellow, who'd stubbornly refused to give his name, had had damn little in the way of possessions. And while no one, certainly not the ex-con, had ever exactly said so, Longarm had gotten the distinct impression that what he had on and with him was all he owned. He would have come out of Canon City—if Canon City it was—with the gun and clothes he'd had when he was processed in and with ten silver dollars to see him on his way.

Yesterday he'd owned the gun, the clothes, and four dollars and—if Longarm remembered right—fourteen cents.

Today he had the gun and the clothes, twelve .38 rimfire cartridges loose in his right-hand pants pocket, eight shotgun shells marked single-ought size on the wadding, and cash totaling 187 dollars and ninety-six cents. Longarm counted it twice to make sure.

If he had to guess—and he supposed he did because this prick wasn't going to tell him—sometime between when Longarm booked him into the jail and this morning when he met his Maker, the man had been paid two hundred dollars and handed a shotgun. And told to go perform a job.

Longarm could well imagine what that job of work was supposed to be.

During the interim the guy had spent, what, seventeen dollars? No, sixteen and change, Longarm amended when he thought about it a little more. Exactly how much didn't matter. Plenty enough anyway for a box of .38s, a box of 12-gauge single-0 buckshot, and an evening of good times.

Longarm stood again and stared down for a moment at the curiously deflated-looking corpse at his feet.

Sixteen dollars' worth of good times.

He kind of doubted it'd been worth it.

The boy Rick pulled up with the wagon, driving his team through the crowd without much regard for giving the men time to get out of the way, and brought the cobs to a halt close to Longarm.

"You, mister, and you. Give me a hand here. We're gonna load the dead man into this wagon. You take the feet, if you please. You, mister, you grab hold of his hand there. I'll get the other'n. Hold your horses steady now, Rick. They're apt to booger once the dust settles an' they get a sniff of the blood. Steady now. Steady. That's good, thanks."

Longarm gave the men who'd helped him a nod of thanks while he made short work of latching the end gate of the wagon in place.

The movement of the body caused some more fluids to be released, and blood began to trickle out of the back of the cargo box. A weak-stomached spectator found that somewhat more than he could handle for some reason and began puking in the grass. The sour smell of his vomit set off a couple others who were standing close by. As far as Longarm was concerned, it'd serve them right if it happened to all of them, but in fact those three were the only ones to show any distress because of the mayhem that had taken place.

"You know the Cargyle jail, Rick? I want you to take me there," Longarm said as he climbed onto the wagon's driving box.

Rick sent an unhappy glance over his shoulder toward the load he was carrying. But a job was a job. And the dead guy was already bleeding all over the place. Rick was going to have to wash the wagon out now whether he completed the job or not. "Yes, sir," he said, and shook his lines to set the team into motion.

Longarm stopped by the Fulton place as they rolled past it, and roused Angela and Buddy from hiding. It appeared that breakfast was going to be later than he'd figured, but he expected they would forgive him for the delay.

153

Then the wagon rolled on. Longarm reached for a cheroot and, his hand steady when he applied the match, settled back on the unpadded seat while the boy Rick took care of the driving.

Chapter 31

The jail was empty this morning. Not even Longarm's pal the coal miner was in residence at the moment. Longarm scowled for a moment. Then grunted. "Back this thing up, will you? Right into the doorway there, just as close as you can get it."

Rick gave him a strange look, but did as Longarm asked. There was no real ditch beside the road to have to negotiate, just a shallow depression that would more or less channel snowmelt and rainwater runoff along the side of the road. The boy swung the wagon away, and backed the team into place with a fair degree of skill.

"That's good," Longarm said when the back of the wagon box was very nearly close enough to the stone wall of the jail to bump into it. "Hold 'em there."

Again the boy's look was questioning. But he didn't voice the questions he so obviously wanted to ask.

While Rick held the horses steady, Longarm unlatched the low tailgate and dropped it.

Without ceremony he reached in and took hold of the dead man's ankle. One good yank and the body slithered out of the wagon and over the edge to fall in a bloody tangle directly in the doorway of the Cargyle jail.

"But . . ." Rick saw the look in Longarm's eye and clamped down hard on whatever protest he might have made. The boy looked quickly away. Longarm walked around to the passenger side of the wagon and climbed onto the box. "Let's go."

"Sir?"

"You heard me. Let's go. Back down to Cletus Terry's saloon." He reached inside his coat for another cheroot.

"But . . ." The kid glanced unhappily over his shoulder. Not that he could see the dead man lying on the stone doorstep back there. That sight would have been obscured by the bed of the wagon. But what he could not see he could all too readily imagine. And what he could imagine was not pleasant to see.

"Don't worry about it, son," Longarm said in a matter-of-fact tone. "Somebody will come along an' notice before it starts to stink too bad."

The boy swallowed hard and looked like he might well follow the example of those grown-ups who'd already donated their breakfasts to the weeds. He got a mite pale and sweaty around the forehead, but was able to control the queasiness. "Y-yessir," he managed. He shook the lines out and wheeled his team back down the canyon toward the gate.

Rick seemed mighty grateful once they reached the saloon and he could get rid of his passenger. Longarm paid him a full dollar for his services—probably it was the hardest money the kid had ever earned—and let him go without the embarrassment of any thanks.

Terry's saloon, Longarm was fairly surprised to see, was open and, despite the hour, doing a thriving business. Longarm kind of thought if he put his mind to it real extra hard he might be able to work out what had given everybody such a thirst so early in the day.

It occurred to him that he'd forgotten something thus far this morning, so he walked over to the cafe and arranged for the helpful fellow there to carry breakfast to Angela and Buddy Fulton. Then Longarm went back to the saloon and ambled inside.

The buzz of the dozens of separate conversations going on at once all stopped abruptly at his entrance.

"Good morning, gents," he said pleasantly enough. He looked the crowd over as he made his way to the bar.

Instead of serving up the usual beer and rum crooks, though, the daytime bartender told him, "Mr. Terry would like to talk with you."

"Oh?"

"The night bartender told him what you said."

"All right, thanks."

"He's in the back. He said if you were to come in—"

"Tell Mr. Terry for me, please, that I'll be at my usual table. Not that I don't trust him, of course. But I'm gettin' kinda tired of being shot at in this town an' don't want to take no more chances. I'm sure he'll understand."

"Yes, sir. Do you, um, still want that beer now?"

"No, but I'd take a coffee if you got any."

"I'll get it for you right away."

Longarm dragged a chair into the corner and leaned against the wall there. The bartender brought the coffee to him, and a small plate of cold ham and crackers too, then disappeared into the back of the place. The barman returned after a couple of minutes, and in another couple of minutes Clete Terry came out with Harry Bolt following close on his heels.

The two helped themselves to seats directly in front of Longarm.

"Tim told me you're wanting—I believe the word he used was 'restitution,' Long."

"That was the word, all right. But it ain't me that oughta be entitled to the recompense."

"Do you mean to tell me that you're expecting me to pay some damn tart like that—whatever the hell her name is—for slapping her around a little?" Terry blurted out.

Longarm smiled at him. And Bolt dug an elbow into his ribs. Cletus Terry coughed into his fist and looked uncomfortable.

"Two hundred," Terry said abruptly.

Longarm's original idea had been to extract a decent year's wage from this asshole. Three hundred sixty dollars, say. That would have been fair payment, he figured. And more than enough for Angela and Buddy to leave Cargyle with if that was what they chose to do.

But now, after this morning, and with the knowledge that whatever amount was finally paid would actually be coming out of Harry Bolt's pocket . . .

"Five hundred," he said without taking time to think over the change.

"That's ridiculous."

"If you say so. But it's what I'll recommend the lady accept. Not a penny less."

"Three hundred," Terry countered.

"Six," Longarm said.

"Three fifty."

"Seven fifty." Longarm's arms were folded and his eyes half closed.

"You son of a bitch."

"Eight hundred."

"Quit dicking around with this, the both of you," Bolt snarled. "Long, you asked for five hundred to begin with."

"That's right, I did."

"Clete, go get the man five hundred out of the safe."

"But, Harry . . ."

"*Do* it!"

Well, Longarm hadn't particularly wondered which of them was in charge here.

Cletus Terry didn't look real happy. But he got up and headed in the direction of the back room.

"Terry," Longarm called out to him before he'd gone more than a few paces. "That's five hundred the lady will be wanting. And a public apology, nice an' loud, that I want to hear."

Terry looked at Bolt. Who merely nodded.

The saloon keeper cussed some, but kept most of it under his breath. He went on toward the back room, leaving Longarm and Harry Bolt alone.

Before Longarm had time to speak Bolt was already leaning forward to explain. "I owe you an apology, Long. You know that don't come easy to me, but I do. I bought a sad story is what it is. The son of a bitch convinced me. He had to be free last night to see his daughter and keep her from making a big mistake. That's what he claimed. He said he'd come here straight from Canon City to find and help his girl. Said he hadn't seen her in fourteen years. Said that was how long he'd been inside. He sounded so plausible, hell, I should have known better. Anyone should have known better. But I didn't. I bought it and he left my jail laughing up his sleeve, I'm sure. Said he'd be there when I opened up first thing this morning. After all, it wasn't much of a charge you had against him. It wasn't like he'd actually done anything. Just threatened to. You and me have done worse than that to each other every time we've seen each other for, what, eight, nine years now and neither one of us has gone to jail over it. I didn't think there was any harm in letting him go take care of his daughter. If he even had a daughter.

"Now this morning I hear he tried to kill you. And had a bunch of cash on him when you checked him out. He only had four dollars or so in his pockets when he left my jail yesterday evening. He even asked me for a loan to help him out. I didn't go that far, of course, but I can tell you he didn't have much on him then. How much was he carrying this morning?"

Longarm told him.

Bolt shook his head. "Near two hundred. And a whole night to spend part of it. He must have been paid two, maybe two hundred fifty dollars for the job then. I really do owe you an apology. And you have it, Long. I'm sorry. I am deeply, truly sorry that that happened this morning. It's my fault."

Longarm was taken completely aback by the apology. There were many things he might have expected this morning from Harry Bolt. An apology wasn't among them. Hell, an apology wouldn't have made his long list of the thousand possibilities most likely.

"And if you're wondering if I might be the one who hired him for the job, well, I can't blame you for thinking it," Bolt went on.

"Actually, Harry, that never crossed my mind."

"No? Shit, Long, I feel practically hurt that you wouldn't think of me. You know I hate your damn guts."

"Sure you do, Harry. An' I hate yours. But what's that got to do with anything? I never thought of you for the job because it ain't your style. You'd shoot me yourself—or try to—if you thought it needed doing. I don't doubt that for a minute. But pay somebody else for the job? I can't see that, Harry. Shit, it'd cost you almost as much to hire somebody as it woulda cost to pay off Mrs. Fulton. As much as it woulda cost if that imbecile Terry knew how to act human today. An' then you'd have somebody walkin' around with knowledge he could hold against you afterward besides. No, Harry, I can't see you for hiring that fella to come after me. You're smarter than that."

"Why, thank you, Custis. Coming from you I take that as a high compliment."

"Well, it ain't intended as one. Just a simple truth."

"So do you have any ideas about who might have wanted you killed here?"

"Besides you and Clete Terry, you mean?" Longarm shook his head. "Can't think of a soul. Not one."

Bolt pursed his lips and pulled at his chin with the fingers of both hands, tugging and stretching the skin there like he was pulling taffy. "I don't suppose the man could have stolen that money and shotgun," he mused aloud. "Then went looking for you for the same reason he braced you yesterday. Pure meanness and a big hate for marshals."

"We're talkin' about human beings here, Harry. That makes anything possible. But I got to tell you that I ain't no believer in coincidence. An' him just happening to luck into a score that'd include a shotgun—that'd stretch things pretty damn far, wouldn't it?"

"Just a thought," Bolt said. "I think maybe—" They were interrupted by a clanging on a stove lid over by the bar.

"Listen up, everybody," Clete Terry was announcing in a loud voice. "I been asked to make an apology about something. A public apology. So all right, damn it. Here goes."

Longarm lighted a cheroot and leaned back to listen to what Mr. Terry had to say on the subject of how to treat women. Even the fallen variety.

Chapter 32

Longarm gave Angela the five hundred dollars in gold coin—
he practically had to beat her up himself in order to get her to
accept the payment—and a complete rundown on the apology
Cletus Terry had made before the saloon full of local men.

"This is enough for Eric and me to get a start somewhere
where they don't know . . . you know . . . somewhere fresh,"
she said, obviously in awe of the amount of money that she
held now in her lap.

"That's kinda what I was hoping you'd want to do," Longarm
admitted.

Angela smiled. Her bruises were still horridly discolored
and her face was lumpy and swollen. But there was nothing
wrong with her eyes, and Longarm found that he liked it
when he saw her smile reach them. "I'm a good seamstress,
you know. Really and truly good. With this much money to
start with I could set up a shop. Not just another shop catering
to ladies, though. There are lots of them everywhere you go.
I could make fancy clothes for children. I'm very, very good
at that anyway. And I think there might be a good market for
that. You know. Something that not everyone is doing. What
do you think, Mr. Long?"

"Sounds fine to me. You'd want to set up someplace where there's lots of rich folks."

"Denver?"

"Maybe. Central City might be better. Lots of money there. And it's close enough that the swells from Denver would take the train out to shop an' buy from you if you was to advertise in the Denver newspapers. Make it, you know, special because of the trip involved. Make it a big deal goin' out there to get the very best in the way of fancy kids' duds."

Angela was beaming now. She clapped her hands in excitement. "This sounds wonderful. Eric? What do you think, dear?"

"Can we take Peppy and my cart?"

She gave Longarm a questioning glance, and he quickly nodded. Hell, it wouldn't cost but a few dollars to haul a pony and cart along with them on the train. Angela had money enough for that and more now.

"Of course we'll take Peppy, darling."

The boy's enthusiasm was quick to join in with his mother's once he had that promise in hand. But then with kids like Rick for pals in Cargyle, it was obvious Buddy wouldn't be leaving anything very dear behind when he shook off the dust of this place.

"And what about you, Mr. Long?"

"Oh, I'll be pulling out soon too. No real point in stayin' now. I don't know who it is that was wantin' me gunned down, but odds are I never will know now. His hired man couldn't do the job, an' I reckon he ain't man enough to try it his own self. I sure ain't gonna sit around here makin' a target of myself while I wait for him to get his nerve up. I got better things to do than that. No, I got done what I needed to here. I'll stay over one more night, then pull out tomorrow."

"Will I, that is to say, will *we* see you again? In Denver perhaps?"

"If you like, Miz Fulton, an' if you're feeling up to the travel, I don't see why we couldn't take the train together as far as Denver. Then when you get settled in Central City, or wherever it is you decide you want to go, you could, like, drop me a note to say where you are. Y'know? And I could maybe stop in sometime. If that'd be all right."

Buddy put his approval on the plan immediately. And vocally. Angela endorsed it as well, but with a look she kept carefully hidden from her son.

"Eric, do you feel up to getting dressed and running an errand?" she said to him.

The boy seemed a mite reluctant to give up his recuperation period. After all, any kid likes to be waited on and fussed over. But with the prospect of moving to a fancy town like Central City—and with Peppy too—he abandoned his invalid status readily enough and hopped out of bed. After all, he hadn't been very badly wounded by those shotgun pellets. It was the status much more than any pain that had kept him bedridden since.

"I want you to run down to Mr. Tankerson's store. Tell him he can come make an offer on the things we won't be taking with us. And mind you tell him he can make part of the payment in kind. We'll be needing crates and packing goods, things like that. That will make it more attractive to him, knowing he can render a part payment in materials. Oh, and you will need to ask someone, Mr. Martinez, I think, about what we will need for Peppy's travel. If we have to carry hay and water or if we will need ropes to tie him in place with. Gracious, there is so much I don't know about travel." A cloud of sadness crossed her battered face. "Your father always used to take care of everything like that, you know."

Neither Angela nor Buddy had ever said much about the boy's father, and Longarm hadn't wanted to ask. Whatever the story was, it was a painful one for both of them. And apparently the man was dead, and not just a runaway who'd grown tired of the responsibilities of heading a family.

Longarm stood and, stretching, gave Buddy a wink. Angela had things under control here now, and Longarm was just underfoot.

Besides, the two of them had had their breakfast this morning, but Longarm never had gotten around to eating yet today.

He figured he could walk down to the cafe—it was lunchtime and soon would be past that—for a bite. Then maybe he'd drop over to the saloon for something to settle his meal with.

After all, for the past couple days he'd been sitting there with a warm beer in front of him but hadn't allowed himself a drop to drink.

The way he saw it he was damn well entitled now if he wanted a shot to warm his belly and maybe a beer to chase that with.

He said his good-byes—neither Angela nor Buddy seemed to notice that he was leaving, they were so wrapped up in their own excited plans—and wandered out into the sunlight of the early afternoon.

Chapter 33

Longarm sat in his usual spot—hell, he'd been in that same chair so much lately that anything else would've felt unnatural—with an empty shot glass and a half-full beer in front of him.

The rotgut whiskey still tasted like wildcat piss, but the beer was going down mighty nice. He lighted up one of his own good cheroots and leaned back to enjoy himself.

Even the sight of Harry Bolt and Clete Terry down at the far end of the bar wasn't enough to make him unhappy. Not now. This business in Cargyle was over and done with as far as he was concerned. He'd done everything here that he had to, and he could leave with a clear conscience. And with Angela Fulton, who was a sweet little woman even if she wasn't much of a looker. Once she healed up and got to feeling herself again he just might . . . no, he damn sure *would* go and look up her and Buddy in Central City. He liked the kid and he liked the mother and he could enjoy seeing more of the both of them. Why, sometime maybe they could all take one of those excursion trains that they ran down to—

Almost without conscious thought he set the beer down onto the table and sat upright.

The young man who'd just walked in didn't fit with this crowd somehow. It wasn't his age. Lots of mining men start out young. In fact probably most of them.

But there was something about him . . . he was too clean, too nicely dressed, looked too much the schoolboy to fit in here with these coal miners.

The young man paused in the doorway and looked slowly around.

That was part of it, Longarm realized. There was a wariness about this fellow that didn't quite fit the rest of his appearance.

He was dressed in a nicely tailored and fairly new suit with a spanking-clean celluloid collar and a carefully tied necktie. He wore a narrow-brimmed hat in the stockman's style, but there was something about him that prevented any possibility that he might be mistaken for a stockman. His shoes were freshly blacked, and there wasn't a hint of sag in his stockings. All in all he was turned out as neat and tidy as a choirboy early on a Sunday morning.

Yet there was that indefinable something about him, something in the cautious way he inspected the room before he committed himself to it, that commanded Longarm's attention.

Longarm looked across the room to where Bolt and Terry were in deep conversation about something. The two of them had their heads together, and were paying no mind to what all was going on around them.

On an impulse Longarm stood and, taking his beer with him, ambled across the room to reach the bar at just about the same time as this young newcomer did. And at the same stretch of bar as well. He stopped beside the young man and nodded to him. "Howdy."

"Hello."

"Buy you a beer, Steve?"

"Yes, thank you." The fellow gave Longarm a quizzical look. "Have we met, perchance?"

"Not that I recall, no."

"Then how—?"

"A shot in the dark." Longarm grinned. "You should excuse the expression."

"I don't know what you mean, sir."

"No, of course you wouldn't."

"You have the advantage of me, sir."

"Oh, yeah. So I do." Longarm introduced himself.

"A federal officer. My, oh, my."

"An' you, of course, would be Steve Reese. How's your papa, Steve?"

"He's holding his own, Marshal. Thank you for asking."

"I hope that treatment in—Scotland, was it?—I hope it helps."

"You're trying to tell me that you know all about my hopes, aren't you."

"I'm trying to tell you, Steve, that you ain't gonna make it. There must be paper out on you in half a dozen different places."

"Really? Am I accused of something then?"

"You know that better'n I do."

"Federal crimes, Marshal?"

"Reckon you know that too."

Reese smiled. "Yes, so I do. I have, shall we say, done my homework, Marshal. And if crimes were committed—which I do not admit, you understand—but if crimes were committed they do not fall under federal jurisdiction."

"You're a cool one, Steve."

"No, Marshal. Merely committed to the pursuit of justice. Notice that I did not say anything about law. Law and justice are unrelated. And the course I seek, sir, is that of the just."

"That so, is it?"

Reese nodded. "Indeed. If you want to know, Marshal, my father is an innocent man. I was there, don't forget. Not that I was allowed to testify during the court-martial. But I was with my father through all those years. I knew. My father knew. His mistake was in his loyalty to men who weren't worthy of the trust he placed in them. He was in charge of supply procurement, you know."

"I heard that, yes."

"He conducted himself honorably and with scrupulous attention to detail. Unfortunately for him there were others, officers who were in charge of the actual disbursement of those supplies, who acted in collusion with several of the Indian agents on the reservations at the time. My father saw that all appropriate materials were made available. All of it of the best possible quality too. Then others took those supplies and sold them on the civilian market. They either took them outright or in some instances replaced them with inferior goods. The Indians who were supposed to receive the supplies received useless goods. Or many times received nothing at all. It couldn't have been done without the cooperation of both the reservation agents and the officers in charge of the actual distribution."

Longarm grunted. What young Reese was telling him was, sadly enough, an all too common tale.

"The saddest thing of all, Marshal, is that my father knew about this. He learned about it at least eight months before charges were filed. Oh, he agonized over that knowledge. And in the end, you see, he decided that he could not bring charges against men who he regarded as his brothers. He pleaded with them to desist. He even threatened to expose them. But in his heart of hearts—he told me this himself—he knew he could never bear to ruin them." Reese's laugh was short and bitter. "They repaid him well for his loyalty. They falsified documents and brought charges against him. For their own crimes. I am sure, we both are sure, they believed if they did not strike first, then he would expose them as he so often threatened he would."

"What about what he knew then? Shouldn't that of been more'n enough of a defense for him?"

"Marshal. Please. Who would have believed him if he had tried to say anything after charges were already pending against him? It would have been taken as a craven attempt to wriggle out from under the truth."

"So he stood there an' took it on the chin?"

"He had no choice, Marshal. Besides, he still believed in his fellow officers. Then. He went to prison still certain that one of his brothers would yet step forward to exonerate him."

Reese snorted. "Brothers indeed. Scrofulous sons of bitches is more like it." The handsome young man brightened and began to smile. "But say, did you know that most of them are dead now?"

"Oh, really?"

"My, yes. There's a delightful irony in it, don't you think?"

"I'd think that only if it happened by accident," Longarm said.

Steven Reese shrugged. "By happenstance or misadventure, I think it hardly matters so long as the end result remains. They all deserved to die, you know. From that pompous Fetterman right on through to the last man on the list."

"Except for your father," Longarm said.

"Yes, of course. Except for him."

"And you intend to see that it works out like that."

"I never said that, did I, Marshal? Please don't assume more than meets the eye. Surely you've been taught that."

"I been taught a lotta things, Steve. Among 'em being that murder is wrong."

"Yes, there are wrongs. And then there are greater wrongs. Who are we to judge which among many wrongs is the greater or the lesser?"

"Me, I don't try to. But I hear tell you sometimes take that chore upon yourself."

"Do you have a warrant for my arrest, Marshal?"

"Well, um, no. Not exactly."

"Then tell me, sir. Is there a point to this conversation?"

"I'd like for there to be, son. I'd sure hell like to talk you out of this scheme of yours. I'd like to see you pull outa here and—I dunno—go visit your papa while you still can. All that money, son, it won't buy him a day more than his appointed time. Ain't that what the Book says? Our days are all numbered an' there's naught we can do to change any least bit of whatever is ordained."

"Do you believe that, Marshal?"

"The question ain't so much what I believe, son, as what's true. So what is it that *you* believe?"

"I believe that my loyalty belongs to my father, Marshal. And to justice. Regardless of law."

"You don't look as hard as you are, y'know that?"

The young man smiled, making him look even younger and more boyish than before. "Yes, in fact I do know that. It has stood me in good stead too, if I do say it."

"Yeah, I'll bet. With that meek an' mild look on you, Steve, I bet you can walk right up to a man an' shoot him between the eyes without him ever once thinking his time had come."

Reese laughed, and in the sound there was an edge of hysteria, or worse, that made Longarm realize for the first time that this gentle veneer the boy wore had no more depth than the clothing on his back.

Beneath the gentle, entirely presentable surface he showed to the world, Steven Reese was crazy as hell. Murderously crazy.

"Steve, what I think I'd best do is ask you to come with me while we check an' see are there any warrants outstanding."

"I thought you said—"

"When I left Denver there was a lawyer, a fella name of Beckwith, who was working on getting one issued."

"Samuel T. Beckwith?" Reese asked. "I remember him. I remember all of them. The bastards. Not good enough to shine my father's boots, those officers. If you only knew."

Longarm looked past Reese toward Harry Bolt, who must have sensed that something was happening here, for now he'd left the table where he'd been talking with Clete Terry and was coming toward Longarm and Reese. The small but deadly little Smith & Wesson revolver was already in his hand. Longarm gave Harry a frown and a quick shake of the head to show that he had this under control. He didn't need any help right now.

"You won't mind if we check with the office in Denver, will you, Steve? I'll get a telegraph message off. We'll have the answer in a couple hours. Then if there's no warrant I won't have no choice but to let you go." Longarm didn't mention that he would be checking for state and territorial warrants in Kansas, Wyoming, Nebraska, and New Mexico as well as for the federal warrants they'd been discussing. Surely someone would have paper outstanding on Reese.

"I haven't violated any federal laws, Marshal. We both know that. And I admit to violating no state laws either."

"Then you an' me will just set an' visit for a while until my answer comes back, an' soon as it does I'll apologize for your trouble an' see you on your way. Now that sounds fair, don't it?"

Reese smiled and bobbed his head. "Yes, Marshal, I have to say that it does."

"All right then. Let's take care of it."

A few feet away Harry Bolt was leaning over the bar in whispered consultation with the bartender. Harry still had the little .32 in his fist.

"If you got a gun on you, Steve, I s'pose you oughta hand it over. Nothing personal, you understand. Just routine."

"Certainly, Marshal. And I don't take it personally, I assure you." The beaming young man pulled his coat open and reached into a hip pocket.

There was a sharp whipcrack of noise from behind him, and the front of Steven Reese's face bulged outward.

Blood and specks of teeth and white bone sprayed forward, settling like a scarlet mist all over Longarm and painting his clothes red.

Reese's blood was blown into Longarm's nose and onto his lips. He could smell the sharp scent of it and taste the salt and copper flavor of it.

Young Steve Reese collapsed before Longarm like a poleaxed shoat, twitched once or twice, and then subsided save for the gurgling of fluids and gases rumbling within the corpse.

"Jesus!" someone nearby muttered, crossing himself and scurrying out of the bar into the afternoon heat.

Chapter 34

Longarm sent Angela Fulton and Buddy on to Denver and Central City without him. He left them at Pueblo and stopped there long enough to transmit two lengthy telegrams, then took the first train west to Canon City and the cold, looming presence of the state penitentiary. The warden there was an old acquaintance if not quite a close friend. Close enough, though, that Longarm could count on his help.

From Canon City Longarm returned to Pueblo and entrained north again to Denver, where Billy Vail's clerk Henry already had part of the information Longarm needed. The rest of it would be in the hands of Sam Beckwith, who was away in Omaha. Longarm fired off a message for the prosecutor and, with Henry's help again, launched his own search for information in the archives of the Federal Building and in the state and old territorial government records of Colorado.

Finally, almost two weeks after he'd left, he headed south again.

As before the train announced the presence of a passenger by blasting the whistle, then dropping him at the spur switch.

As before Rick came out with his wagon to pick up the fare. This time, however, there was no need for him to race Buddy and Peppy for the privilege.

"I thought you was gone, mister."

"An' so I was. Now I'm back. D'you want my business or not?"

"I want your business, sure."

"Then load my things in an' let's go."

"Yessir."

Now that it was familiar to him the ride to Cargyle seemed short. He had Rick drop him outside Clete Terry's—and Harry Bolt's—saloon.

"Are you looking for a place to stay the night, mister?"

"Not this time. I'll tend to my business and be gone before dark, more'n likely. But don't go off too far. I'll be wanting a ride back out in time to catch the eight-oh-five northbound."

"You want I should look after your saddle and bag until then, mister?"

"That'd be good, thanks." Longarm dragged his Winchester from its scabbard strapped to his saddle, but left everything else in the boy's wagon.

Rick eyed the rifle. "Mister, you ain't . . ."

"Yes, son?"

"Never mind. Never you mind, mister." The boy rolled his eyes and got the hell out of there quick like he thought guns might start going off at any moment.

Longarm grunted softly under his breath and went inside the saloon.

"I can't say I expected to see you back here, Marshal," the daytime bartender said, greeting him.

"In my line, friend, a man never knows."

"I suppose that's true."

"You wouldn't happen to know where I can find Chief Bolt, would you?"

"Yes, sir, he and Mr. Terry are in the back."

"Ask the chief to join me out here, would you, please?"

"Sure thing, Marshal. You want a beer or anything while you're waiting?"

"No, thanks, I'm fine."

The bartender nodded and, first checking to make sure no one needed his immediate attention at the bar, went into the back of the saloon.

Longarm wandered over to the corner where he'd spent so many hours before. The table he was used to had been dragged a short distance away, and the chairs were not arranged to his liking. He left the table where it was, but found the chair he favored and pulled it over against the wall, dropping into it with the Winchester laid across his lap.

Harry Bolt came out in a minute or so, Clete Terry with him. The two men stopped at the bar to draw beers for themselves, then carried those and a plate of pickled eggs over to join Longarm in the corner.

"If this is about that Reese boy, Long, my story hasn't changed. I told you the truth. I seen he was reaching for a gun and didn't know he was fixing to hand it over to you peaceful. Which maybe he was and maybe he wasn't. So I shot. I did it to protect a fellow peace officer, and I'd do it again. I suppose, though, you'll be wanting a written statement to that effect. Is that what you've come for?"

"Actually, Harry, what I come here about don't have nothing to do with Steve Reese's murder."

Bolt raised an eyebrow and began to look a mite prickly. "I don't much care for your use of the word murder there, Long."

"That's all right, Harry. You're entitled to your feelings on the subject." Longarm stuck a cheroot between his teeth and flicked a match into flame. He held the flame to the end of the cigar and took his time about building a coal, then shook the match out and tossed it toward a cuspidor in the corner. He kept the cheroot in his teeth and laid his hand onto the grip of the Winchester.

"If you'd be more comfortable," Longarm offered, "I could call you Dennis instead of Harry."

"What?"

"Dennis Connor O'Dell is the long of it, I believe."

"Who are you talking about, Long? Have you gone crazy in the head here?"

"All these years. Just think of it, Dennis. You've gotten away with it for all these years."

"I don't know—"

"Yes, you do, Dennis. What happened? Did Harry Bolt serve that warrant on you? It was the last he ever signed out. We looked it up. And it was never returned. Paper on Dennis Connor O'Dell, George Timothy Ward, and James Leon Fowler. Harry Bolt, the real Harry Bolt that is, was never seen again afterward. Not by anybody who'd known him before, though someone calling himself Harry Bolt showed up in southern Colorado soon afterward. George Ward was killed a couple years ago in Arizona. Did you know that? And James Leon Fowler died right here about two weeks back. I know because I killed him myself. More to the point, Dennis—or if you wouldn't mind—Harry. I've got in such a habit of calling you by that name that it's hard to quit now that I know different. Anyway, that was your old pard who showed up here. What was it, Harry? Dennis? Did he come here by accident an' just happen to recognize you? Or had he kept track of you all that time till he got outa the pen?"

"I don't know what you're—"

'Of course you know, Dennis. Harry. You're the one who set Fowler up to kill me, of course. Shit, it was the smart thing for you to do. Which I finally recognized once I peached to what had happened all those years ago. The real Harry Bolt arrested you but somehow you managed to kill him. An' instead of staying on the run as Dennis O'Dell with a price on your head, you took Harry Bolt's papers an' pretended you was him. Got away with it all this time too, and would've got away with it for who knows how much longer except all of a sudden there was two different threats that could expose you.

One was James Leon Fowler, who knew you from back when. The other was Steven Reese, who didn't know you at all.

"With Fowler it was easy. You turned him outa the jail that night, handed him a shotgun, an' sicced him onto me. Like I said, Harry. Dennis. It was smart. No matter what Fowler done, you won. If he killed me, then I wasn't no threat to learn the truth from Reese, who you already knew was supposed to be on his way to find Harry Bolt. An' if I killed Fowler, then Fowler wasn't no threat to expose you as Dennis O'Dell. So you came out ahead no matter what happened.

"Another thing I've figured out this past couple weeks, Harry—excuse me, Dennis—is that if I'd delivered the message an' gone right back to Denver there wouldn't have been no problem for you. Or anybody else. Young Reese would have come here, tracked you down, and found out you didn't look anything like his Harry Bolt. So he would have gone off looking someplace else for the officer he'd known when he was a kid. But thanks to your muscle-headed friend there, I hung around town a few days longer than I otherwise woulda, an' so I was a danger to you. What if Reese came an' I found out he didn't recognize you? That's what happened, of course. I'd of let it all pass after Fowler was dead except for Reese walking in here an' looking around." Longarm smiled around the end of his cheroot. "Looked right at you, Harry. An' right on by. He'd of reacted if he'd seen Harry Bolt in this room here. But he didn't. All he'd seen was a bunch of strangers. That's why he had to die, Harry. That's why you had to kill him before he could complain to me about not finding Harry Bolt here in Cargyle where Harry Bolt was s'posed to be all this time."

"You're crazy, Long. You been drinking Chinese medicines or something."

"Really, Dennis? You'll swear to that?"

"Hell, yes, I will."

"That's good, Dennis. Because there's a man on his way

right now who served in the army with his brother officer Harry Bolt. The man's name is Beckwith. He's a lawyer now. An assistant to the United States attorney in the Denver district. He says he won't have no trouble recognizing Harry Bolt." That part was a bit of a lie. Beckwith was still in Omaha and would be needed there for some weeks more. Billy Vail had agreed with Longarm, though, that Harry Bolt—or Dennis O'Dell—should be taken quickly, before something might spook him and make him turn rabbit on them. They hadn't wanted to risk him getting away yet another time.

"Harry?" Clete Terry whined. "What the hell is he talking about, Harry?"

"Shut up, Clete."

"Haven't you been listening, Cletus? Your pal here isn't Harry after all. He's Dennis. And he's still wanted on charges of mail theft, robbery, murder—there's probably more paper still outstanding on him. But that's all right. We got plenty of time to look it all up an' find out just how many different jurisdictions want to file charges against him."

"Harry? Is he telling me the truth, Harry?"

"He's lying, Clete. He's always wanted a chance to get back at me. Ever since I took his woman away from him years and years ago. He's jealous of me, Clete. And I think it's time to put a stop to this. Are you with me, Clete? Will you back me here?"

"Anything you say, Harry. You know that."

"Kill him, Clete! Kill him now."

Harry Bolt—Dennis O'Dell—was already moving, rolling out of his chair and placing Clete Terry's bulk between him and Longarm.

Terry was moving too. But unlike Bolt or Longarm, Cletus Terry thought in terms of muscle and steel. He reached not for a gun but for a knife.

Longarm ignored Terry. The threat came from Bolt after all. O'Dell, dammit. Dennis O'Dell.

179

He earred back the hammer of the Winchester and sent a slug into Harry Bolt's stomach.

Unfortunately for Clete Terry, the bullet had to pass through his thigh in order to reach Bolt.

Longarm didn't stop to worry about that. He levered the Winchester and fired again. If he gave Harry Bolt time to get that shit-eating little Smith into action, Longarm was a dead man, and he knew it. Harry—Dennis—wasn't fast, but he was hell for accurate.

Longarm quit fooling with the slow-to-load Winchester and spun out of his chair, palming his revolver as he moved.

Harry was down but he was still game. He slid underneath Clete Terry's chair, using Terry's body for cover.

Longarm saw the nickel flash of Harry's gun.

Longarm's Colt roared first. A .44 slug grazed Terry, causing the big man to scream in pain, and ripped through Harry Bolt's gun arm.

"You're done, Harry. Give it up now."

"Screw you, Long."

"Leave be, Harry. There's nothing left to fight for."

The Smith & Wesson lay on the saloon floor, its nickel plating dulled by blood and clinging sawdust.

Bolt—O'Dell—gritted his teeth and shifted his weight onto the right arm that Longarm's bullet had shattered.

"Leave be, Harry. I'm asking you nice. Leave be."

"The hell with you, asshole."

He picked up the .32 in his left hand.

Longarm took careful aim. And shot him high in the forehead, his bullet neatly centered between Harry Bolt's eyes and slightly above them.

"My God," Cletus Terry said, turning away and vomiting in the blood and brains already on the floor there.

"Yeah," Longarm mumbled. "There ain't no other chance for mercy, is there?"

He looked quickly toward the men at the bar. But no one

there seemed interested in joining the fuss.

He drew smoke from his cheroot deep into his lungs and slowly exhaled, then pulled the railroad-quality Ingersoll out of his watch pocket and checked the time. There was no hurry. Not now. He had plenty of time to make the four-twelve northbound. He wouldn't have to wait for the late train after all.

Watch for

LONGARM AND THE DRIFTING BADGE

185th novel in the bold LONGARM series
from Jove

Coming in May!

A special offer for people who enjoy reading the best Westerns published today.

WESTERNS!

NO OBLIGATION

Mail the coupon below

To start your subscription and receive 2 FREE WESTERNS, fill out the coupon below and mail it today. We'll send your first shipment which includes 2 FREE BOOKS as soon as we receive it.

Mail To: **True Value Home Subscription Services, Inc. P.O. Box 5235**
120 Brighton Road, Clifton, New Jersey 07015-5235

YES! I want to start reviewing the very best Westerns being published today. Send me my first shipment of 6 Westerns for me to preview FREE for 10 days. If I decide to keep them, I'll pay for just 4 of the books at the low subscriber price of $2.75 each; a total $11.00 (a $21.00 value). Then each month I'll receive the 6 newest and best Westerns to preview Free for 10 days. If I'm not satisfied I may return them within 10 days and owe nothing. Otherwise I'll be billed at the special low subscriber rate of $2.75 each; a total of $16.50 (at least a $21.00 value) and save $4.50 off the publishers price. There are never any shipping, handling or other hidden charges. I understand I am under no obligation to purchase any number of books and I can cancel my subscription at any time, no questions asked. In any case the 2 FREE books are mine to keep.

Name _____

Street Address _____ Apt. No. _____

City _____ State _____ Zip Code _____

Telephone _____

Signature _____
(if under 18 parent or guardian must sign)

Terms and prices subject to change. Orders subject
to acceptance by True Value Home Subscription
Services, Inc.

11356-5